D0927052

The *Missing Head*
of Damasceno Monteiro

Also by Antonio Tabucchi

THE EDGE OF THE HORIZON

INDIAN NOCTURNE

LETTER FROM CASABLANCA

LITTLE MISUNDERSTANDINGS OF NO IMPORTANCE

PEREIRA DECLARES

REQUIEM

The Missing Head

of Damasceno Monteiro

Antonio Tabucchi

Translated by
J. C. PATRICK

A NEW DIRECTIONS BOOK

Copyright © 1997 by Giangiacomo Feltrinelli Editore
Copyright © 1999 by J. C. Patrick

All rights reserved. Except for brief passages quoted in a newspaper,
magazine, radio, or television review, no part of this book may be
reproduced in any form or by any means, electronic or mechanical,
including photocopying and recording, or by any information storage
and retrieval system, without permission in writing from the Publisher.

Published under the title *La Testa perduta di Damasceno Monteiro* by
Giangiacomo Feltrinelli, Milan, 1997. This translation is published
by arrangement with the Harvill Press, London.

Manufactured in the United States of America
New Directions Books are printed on acid-free paper.
Published simultaneously in Canada by Penguin Books Canada Limited

Library of Congress Cataloging-in-Publication Data
Tabucchi, Antonio, 1943–
    [Testa perduta di Damasceno Monteiro. English]
    The missing head / Antonio Tabucchi ; translated by J. C. Patrick.
        p.   cm.
    ISBN 0-8112-1393-5 (alk. paper)
    I. Patrick, J. C.   II. Title.
PQ4880.A24T4713   1999
853'.914—dc21   98-31263
                                                       CIP

New Directions books are published for James Laughlin
by New Directions Publishing Corporation
80 Eighth Avenue, New York

SCIENCE FICTION

O marciano encontropu-me na rua
e teve medo de minha impossibilidade humana
O marciano encontropu-me na rua
e teve medo de minha impossibilidade humana

                              Carlos Drummond de Andrade

The Martian met me in the street
and was frightened by the possibility of my being human
How can a being exist, he wondered, who invests
the business of existing with so huge a denial of existence?

One

MANOLO THE GYPSY OPENED HIS EYES, peered at the dim light creeping through the cracks in his hovel, and got to his feet trying not to make a sound. He had no need to dress because he slept fully clothed, and the orange jacket given him the year before by Agostinho da Silva, known as Franz the German, tamer of toothless lions in the Wonder Circus, now served him for both day and night. In the faint glimmer of dawn he groped around for the battered sandals-cum-slippers that were his only footwear. He found them and slid his feet in. He knew every inch of the hut, and could move about in its murk knowing perfectly well where its few wretched sticks of furniture were. He took a confident step towards the door, and in so doing his right foot clashed against an oil-lamp standing on the floor.

Damn the woman! exclaimed Manolo between his teeth. He was of course referring to his wife, who the previous evening had insisted on leaving this lamp beside her bed on the pretext that the blackness of night gave her nightmares and she dreamt of her dead. If she kept the flame burning as low as can be, she said, the ghosts of her dead dared not to haunt her, and so she could sleep in peace.

"And what is El Rey about at this hour of the morning, O afflicted spirit of our Andalusian dead?"

His wife's voice was muffled and drowsy, as it is with anyone still half asleep. She always spoke to him in *geringonça*, a hotchpotch of Romany, Portuguese and Andalusian. And she called him El Rey—the King.

King of a heap of shit, Manolo felt the urge to answer, but he said nothing. King of a shitheap. To be sure he had once been El Rey, when the gypsies were honored, when his people freely roamed the plains of Andalusia, when they made copper trinkets to sell in the villages and dressed in black and wore fine felt hats, and their knives were not weapons to fight for your life with, but peerless treasures fashioned in chased silver. Yes, those were the days of El Rey. But now? Now that they were forced to wander, now that Spain made their lives impossible, and in Portugal, their place of refuge, things were perhaps even worse, now that they no longer had the means of making trinkets and mantillas, now that they had to shift for themselves as best they could with begging and petty theft, what sort of a fucking king was he, Manolo the Gypsy? King of a shitheap, is what he repeated to himself.

The Town Council had granted him that litter-strewn patch of land on the outskirts of town, just beyond the last outlying villas, but merely as an act of charity. He would never forget the face of the town clerk who signed the concession, with an air of condescension together with commiseration, for a twelve-month grant of land at peppercorn rent. . . . and let Manolo remember that. The Council made no commitment to provide commodities of any kind, not so much as water and electricity, and as for shitting they could do it in the woods, after all gypsies were used to that, and they would manure the soil, and they must be careful, because the police were on to their small traffickings, and were keeping their eyes peeled.

King of a shitheap, thought Manolo, with those pasteboard hovels roofed with galvanized iron, streaming with damp in winter and ovens in summer. The dry, spick and span grottoes of the Granada of his youth no longer existed, this place here was a refugee camp, or worse, a concentration camp, thought Manolo, king of a shitheap.

"What is El Rey about at this hour of the morning, O afflicted spirit of our Andalusian dead?"

His wife was now well awake, her eyes wide open. With her grey hair spread over her breast, as she always arranged it for sleep after removing all the hairpins, and that pink nightgown she slept in, she looked like a ghost herself.

"I'm off to have a piss," replied Manolo curtly.

"Best thing for you," said his wife.

Manolo shifted his penis inside his underpants, because it was swollen and hard and pressing on his testicles enough to hurt.

"I'd still be able to finfar," he said, "I wake up like this every morning, with my *mangalho* as taut as a rope, yes I'd still be able to *finfar*."

"It's your bladder," said his wife, "you're old, Rey, you think you're young but you're old, even older than I."

"I'd still be able to *finfar*," retorted Manolo, "but I can't *finfar* you, your cunt's full of spiders' webs."

"Then off you go and piss," said his wife to end the matter.

Manolo scratched at his head. For some days he had been suffering from a rash that started at the nape of his neck and spread up into his hair, and it itched intolerably.

"Shall I take Manolito?" he whispered to his wife.

"Leave the poor child to sleep," she replied.

"Manolito likes having a piss with his grand-dad," claimed Manolo.

He looked over towards the camp bed on which Manolito was sleeping and felt a surge of tenderness. Manolito was eight years old. He was all that was left to him of his descendants. He did not even look like a gypsy. He had straight black hair, to be sure, like that of a true gypsy, but he also had blue-green eyes, as must have been those of his mother, whom Manolo had never met. His son Paco, his only son, had fathered him on a prostitute from Faro, an English girl he said, who was walking the streets of Gibraltar when Paco had started pimping for her. Then the girl had been packed off to England by the police, and Paco had found himself saddled with the child. He in turn had dumped him on the grandparents, having an important business deal to bring off in Algarve, he was in the cigarette-smuggling racket. But from that bit of business he never returned.

"He likes seeing the sunrise," insisted Manolo stubbornly.

"Let him sleep, poor child," replied his wife, "it's scarcely dawn yet, have you no heart?—go and empty your bladder."

MANOLO THE GYPSY opened the door of the hut and went out into the morning air. The compound ringed round by the huts was deserted, the whole encampment sleeping. The mongrel cur, which by sheer persistence had got itself adopted by the community, rose from its bed on a sand-heap and bounded up wagging its tail. Manolo clicked his fingers and it stood on its hind legs, wagging its tail even more. With the little dog at his heels Manolo crossed the compound and took the path alongside the pinewood sloping down towards the Douro. It was only a few hectares, grandiloquently entitled "Municipal Park," and officially publicized blazoned forth as the "green lung" of the town. In fact it was nothing but an abandoned area, with no patrols and no superintendence. Every morning Manolo found the place littered with condoms and syringes which the Council wouldn't move a finger to clean out.

He started down the little path hemmed in with dense clumps of broom. It was August, and the broom for some reason was flowering on as if it were springtime. Manolo sniffed at the air with expertise. In the course of his life in the wilds he had learnt to distinguish all the many odors of nature. He counted the broom, lavender, rosemary, and so many others.

Beneath him, at the foot of the hill, the River Douro glittered in the slanting rays of the sun which was emerging from the hills. Two or three barges were on their way downstream to Oporto. Their sails swollen with wind, they nevertheless appeared motionless on the winding ribbon of the river. Manolo knew they were carrying great casks of wine to the vast wineries of the city, wine that would be matured, bottled, and labeled as "Port," and make its way all over the world. Manolo felt an enormous yearning for the great world which he had never seen, for distant harbors in foreign climes with cloudy skies, where the mists swirled in as they had in a film he had once seen. But he knew only the blinding white Iberian light of his native Andalusia, and now the dazzle of Portugal, the whitewashed houses, the stray curs, the groves of cork-oaks and the cops who sent him packing wherever he was.

For his piss he had chosen a massive oak that cast its great shadow over a grassy clearing just on the verge of the pines. Who knows why it gave him a sense of comfort to piss against the trunk of that tree, perhaps because it was very much older than he was, and Manolo liked to think there were living things in the world older than him, even if they were only trees. The fact is that it made him feel at his ease, and filled with peace, in harmony with himself and with the universe. So he walked up to the great trunk and urinated with relief. And at that moment he saw a shoe.

What particularly caught his eye was that it did not appear to be an old, cast-off shoe, such as was frequently to be found in that area, but a brightly polished shoe which seemed to him to be made of goatskin, pointing upwards as if there were a foot inside it. And it emerged from beneath a bush.

Manolo approached with caution. Experience told him that it could be a drunkard, or else a delinquent in ambush. He took a look over the tops of the bushes but could see nothing. Then he picked up a stout stick and started to part the bushes this way and that. From the shoe, which turned out to be an ankle-boot, he picked his way to a pair of legs clad in tight-fitting jeans. Manolo's eyes got as far as the waist and there they paused. The belt was made of light-colored leather, with a large silver buckle bearing the image of a horse's head and the inscription "Texas Ranch." With difficulty Manolo sought to decipher the words and impress them well on his memory. Then, still parting the bushes with his stick, he continued his inspection. The trunk of the body was dressed in a blue, short-sleeved T-shirt on which was printed a phrase in some foreign language—Stones of Portugal—which Manolo looked at for a long time to impress this also on his memory. Using his stick he continued his inspection with calm and with caution, as if afraid of hurting that body lying belly upwards in the bushes. He reached the neck, at which point he could go no further. Because the body had no head. There was a clean cut which had caused little bleeding, just a few dark clots on which the flies were buzzing. Manolo withdrew his stick and allowed the bushes to cover the pathetic object. A few steps away he sat down with his back against the big oak and set himself to thinking. To assist thought he took out his pipe and filled it with the tobacco from some *Definitivos* cigarettes, which he picked carefully apart. At one time he liked to smoke shag, but now it was too expensive for him, and he had to fall back on unpicking cigarettes of black tobacco that he bought a few at a time at the shop of a certain Francisco, known as Shittipants, because he walked with his buttocks clenched together as if he were about to shit himself. Manolo filled his pipe, took a few puffs and pondered. He pondered over what he had discovered and decided that there was no need to go back and take a second look. What he had seen was more than enough. And meanwhile time was passing, the cicadas had begun their intolerable chirring and the air around was heavy with the scent of lavender and rosemary. Beneath him stretched the glittering ribbon of the river, a warm, light breeze had sprung up and the shadows of the trees were growing shorter. It occurred to Manolo how lucky it was that he had not brought his grandson. Children ought not to see such horrors, he thought, not even gypsy children. He wondered what time it was and enquired of the sun. Only then did he realize that the shade had shifted, that the sun was shining full on him and he was bathed in sweat. He got wearily to his feet and set off back to the encampment.

There was a lot of activity in the compound at that hour. The old women were washing the infants in tubs and the young mothers were cooking. People hailed Manolo as he passed but he scarcely noticed them. He entered his hut. His wife was dressing up Manolito in an old Andalusian costume, because the community had decided to send the children to sell flowers in Oporto, and it made more impression if they were decked out in traditional costume.

"I've found a dead man in the pinewood," said Manolo softly.

His wife did not catch his meaning. She was combing Manolito's hair and smarming it with brilliantine.

"What was that, Rey?" asked the old woman.

"A corpse, right near the oak."

"Let it rot," replied his wife, "everything around here's rotten."

"There's no head," said Manolo, "they've cut it clean off, *chop!*"

He made a gesture as if chopping his own head off. The old woman stared at him wide-eyed.

"What do you mean?" she asked.

Manolo repeated his gesture: *chop!*

The old woman straightened up and sent Manolito away. "You must go to the police," she said firmly.

Manolo gave her an almost pitying look:

"El Rey does not go to the police," he said with pride, "Manolo of the free gypsies of Spain and Portugal does not enter a police station."

"What's to be done then?" asked the old woman.

"They will be informed by Senhor Francisco," replied Manolo. "Shittipants has a telephone and is always on to the police. Let him tell them, since they're on such friendly terms."

The old woman gave him a worried look and said nothing. Manolo stood up and opened the door of the hut. When he was in the doorway, silhouetted against the full light of day, his wife said:

"You owe him two thousand escudos, Rey, he gave you two bottles of aqua-vitae and put it on your tab."

"Who cares about two bottles of *giripiti*," replied Manolo. "Let him go fuck himself."

Two

FIRMINO WAS HELD UP AT THE traffic light at Largo do
Rato. It was an interminable red light, he knew, and the impa-
tient taxi behind him was practically nudging his back
bumper. Firmino knew that one must be very patient about
the works undertaken by a Council that promised people a
clean and tidy city, and was straining every nerve to make it
the venue of the International Exhibition. This would be a
world event, declared the posters erected at all the neuralgic
points in the traffic, one of those events which would raise Lisbon to the status of a City of the Future. For the moment
Firmino knew only what his immediate future was to be, and
knew no other. It was to wait for at least five minutes at the
light, until the excavator shifted out of the way, and even if the
light turned green there was no means of moving, you still had
to wait. He therefore resigned himself, lit one of the Multifilter
cigarettes sent him by a Swiss friend, tuned the radio in to the
program "Our Listeners Ask Us," just to find out what was
going on, and glanced up at the electronic clock at the top of
the building opposite. It said two o'clock in the afternoon and
gave a temperature reading of one hundred and four degrees.
Well after all, it was August.

Firmino was on his way back from a week's holiday with
his girlfriend in a little village in Alentejo, and bracing days

they had been, even if they had found the tides pretty fierce. However, as always before, Alentejo had not let him down. They had found farmhouse accommodation right on the coast, the owners were German, only nine rooms, and then there were the pinewoods, the beach to themselves, love-play in the open air and local cooking. He took a look at himself in the rear-view mirror: he had a fine tan, he was feeling in good shape, he didn't give a damn about the International Exhibition and was keen to get back to his job on the newspaper. Nor was it only keenness, it was sheer necessity. For his holiday he had spent his previous month's wages down to the last penny.

The light went green, the bulldozer pulled aside and Firmino moved on. He turned off the square at Rua Alexandre Herculano and then took the Avenida da Liberdade. At the Saldanha he found himself in a bottleneck. There had been an accident in the midstream of traffic and all the cars were edging to squeeze into the side lanes. Firmino selected the lane reserved for buses, hoping there were no traffic police in the immediate vicinity. He had recently done some sums with Catarina and realized that fines accounted for ten per cent of his meager monthly salary. But maybe at two in the afternoon in that heat there wouldn't be any traffic cops along the avenue. If there were it was just too bad. When he drove past the National Library he could not help slowing up a little to give it a nostalgic glance. He thought of the afternoons spent in the reading room studying the novels of Elio Vittorini and his vague project of writing a critical essay to be called "The Influence of Vittorini on the Post-War Portuguese Novel." And with that nostalgia came the smell of salt cod frying in the Library's self-service canteen where he had lunched for weeks on end. Ah, salt cod and Vittorini! But the project had so far remained merely a project. Who knows, maybe he would take it up again when he had a little time to spare.

He arrived at the Lumiar and skirted the buildings of the Holiday Inn. A horrible monster. Middle-class Americans disembarked there looking for picturesque Old Lisbon and found themselves on the contrary plumb in the middle of a neighborhood ravaged by new buildings plus the flyover to the airport and the outer beltway. Finding a parking space was always a problem. He pulled in facing a block of flats with an electronic gate, doing his best not to obstruct the entrance. His car stuck out a good half-meter, but to hell with it. If they towed it away his fine-quota would go up by at least two per cent, which meant that he would be unable to buy the last volume of the *Grande Dizionario della Lingua Italiana*, an essential tool for the study of Vittorini. Oh well!

A few meters away loomed the newspaper building, a hideous, vulgar cement edifice built in the 1970s and completely devoid of feature. Most floors were occupied by work-a-day people with jobs in the center, who used their apartments only as dormitories. To give a touch of color to the dismal balconies some of the tenants had installed a sun-umbrella and plastic garden chairs. On the topmost balcony, quite in contrast with such bourgeois embellishments, was an eye-catching placard announcing in vermilion lettering: **O ACONTECIMENTO: "What every citizen needs to know."**

This was his paper, and he made his way there in buoyant spirits. He was aware that he had to face the bosomy and paralyzed telephonist who from her wheelchair directed all the sections of the newspaper, that before reaching his cubbyhole he had to get past the desk of Dr. Silva, head of the editorial staff, who used his mother's surname, Huppert, because a French name was more stylish, and that even when he had gained his own desk he would feel the usual intolerable claustrophobia he always felt, because the cubicle with fake walls in which they had confined him had no window. Firmino knew all this, yet he pressed on with buoyant heart.

The paralytic lady had fallen asleep in her wheelchair. Before her abundant breast was a small, empty tinfoil container with greasy edges. It had been her lunch, delivered by the fastfood at the corner. Firmino walked past her with some relief and entered the elevator. It didn't have any doors, like a freight elevator. Beneath the buttons was a metal plaque engraved with the words "Use of this elevator is forbidden to unaccompanied minors." Beside this, in felt pen, someone had scrawled: Fuck you. By way of compensation the architect who had dreamt up this peerless building had sought to cheer the occupants of the elevator with music piped through a miniature loudspeaker. It was always the same tune: "Strangers in the Night." At the third floor the elevator came to a halt. There entered an elderly lady with a dyed perm which suffused a horrendous perfume.

"Going down?" asked the lady without so much as a nod.

"Going up," replied Firmino.

"I'm going down," said the lady curtly. And she pressed the down button.

Firmino resigned himself and down he went, the lady walked off without so much as a good-day and he went up. When he reached the fourth floor he stood for one disconcerted moment on the landing. What to do? he wondered. What if he had gone to the airport and got on a flight to Paris? Paris, the great magazines, the special correspondents, all those trips the world over. Like a complete cosmopolitan journalist. Notions like this sometimes came to him, the urge to change his life once and for all, a radical choice, a sudden impulse. But the problem was that he didn't have a bean and air tickets run into money. So does Paris. Firmino pushed open the door and went in.

The office premises were what is called open-plan. But originally, of course, they had not been designed as such. They had been converted by knocking down the dividing walls of the apartment, easy enough to demolish since they were made of hollow bricks. This had all been thought up by the firm previously occupying the premises, exporting tinned tuna-fish, and having inherited them in that condition the Editor had made the best of a bad job.

There was no one sitting at the two desks facing the entrance. The first was usually occupied by a mature spinster who acted as secretary, the other by a journalist who worked at the only computer the paper possessed. The third desk was that of Senhor Silva, or rather Huppert, as he signed his articles for the paper.

"Good afternoon, Senhor Silva," said Firmino amiably.

Senhor Silva eyed him with some severity.

"The Editor is furious," he said between his teeth.

"Why is that?" asked Firmino.

"Because he didn't know how to contact you."

"But I was at the sea," explained Firmino.

"You can't go to the sea in times like these," said Senhor Silva acidly. He then pronounced his pet phrase: *mala tempora currunt.*

"That's all very well," returned Firmino, "but I was only supposed to be back tomorrow."

Senhor Silva made no answer, but motioned towards the frosted-glass door of the Editor's little office.

Firmino knocked and breezed straight in. The Editor was on the telephone and gestured to him to wait. Firmino closed the door and remained standing. It was stiflingly hot in that little room and the air conditioner was turned off. Yet the Edi-

tor was dressed in an impeccable grey jacket and wearing a tie.
Also a white shirt. He hung up and raked Firmino from stem
to stern.

"Where were you holing out?" he demanded irritably.

"Alentejo," answered Firmino.

"What were you doing in Alentejo?" demanded the Editor
more irritably still.

"I am on holiday," pointed out Firmino, "and my holiday
doesn't end until tomorrow, I've called in at the paper simply
to know if there's anything new, and whether I can make myself useful."

"You're not useful," snapped the Editor, "you're indispensable, and you're leaving on the six o'clock train."

It occurred to Firmino that it might be better to sit down.
He did so, and lit a cigarette.

"Where to?" he asked imperturbably.

"To Oporto of course," replied the Editor in a neutral
voice.

"Why of course?" asked Firmino, attempting to adopt the
same neutral tone.

"Because there's been a bit of dirty work up there," said the
Editor, "the sort of thing that's going to cause rivers of ink to
flow."

"Can't our man in Oporto cope with it?" asked Firmino.

"No he can't, this is big stuff," stated the Editor.

"Then send Senhor Silva," replied Firmino calmly, "he
likes traveling, and moreover he'll be able to sign the thing
with his French name."

"He runs Editorial," said the Editor, "his job is to edit the
rubbish sent in by the various correspondents. The special correspondent is you."

"But I've only just finished with the woman stabbed by her
husband in Coimbra," protested Firmino, "and that was only

ten days ago, just before my holiday. I spent a whole afternoon in the morgue in Coimbra listening to the police surgeon's evidence."

"Too bad," snapped the Editor, "our special correspondent is you and nobody else. Apart from that, it's already arranged, I've booked you into a pension in Oporto for a week, and that's just to start with, because this case is going to drag on."

Firmino took a little time off to marshal his thoughts. He would have dearly liked to say that he had no love for the city of Oporto, that in Oporto they ate almost nothing but tripe *à la mode d'Oporto* and that tripe made him sick, that Oporto was cursed by sweltering damp heat, that the pension he had been booked in to was doubtless a frightful dump with a bathroom on the landing and that he would die of sheer melancholy. But instead of all this he said:

"Sir, I have to finish my study of the Post-War Portuguese novel, it's a very important thing for me, and anyway I have already signed a contract with the publisher."

"It's a nasty business," cut in the Editor, "a mystery that has to be solved, the public has its tongue hanging out, it's the talk of the day."

The Editor lit a cigarette, lowered his voice as if confessing a secret, and murmured: "They have discovered a headless corpse in the vicinity of Matosinhos, it is still unidentified, it was found by a gypsy, Manolo by name, who gave a muddled account of it to the police, and no one has managed to get another word out of him. He lives in an encampment on the outskirts of Oporto, and it's up to you to search him out and interview him. It'll be the scoop of the week."

The Editor now appeared to be less flustered, as if for him the case had already been solved. He opened a drawer and took out some papers.

"Here's the address of the pension," he added, "it's not a

luxury hotel, but Dona Rosa is a perfect gem, I've known her for thirty years. And here is your check for board, lodging and expenses for one week. If something extra crops up, put it on the bill. And don't forget, the train leaves at six."

Three

WHO KNOWS WHY HE HAD always disliked Oporto?
Firmino thought about this. His taxi was crossing the Praça
da Batalha, a fine square, austere in the English manner.
Oporto did in fact have an English air to it, with its grey stone
Victorian façades and people walking in such orderly fashion
along the streets. Could it be, wondered Firmino, that I don't
feel at ease with the English? Possibly, but it wasn't the main
reason. The one time he'd been in London he had felt perfectly
at home. Obviously Oporto wasn't London, it was merely an
imitation of London, but maybe even this wasn't the reason,
decided Firmino. And he thought back to his childhood, and
his uncles and aunts in Oporto where his parents unfailingly
took him every Christmas holiday. Grim, those Christmases.
They flooded back into Firmino's mind as if they had happened the day before. He saw Aunt Pitù and Uncle Nuno, herself tall and lean and always dressed in black, with a cameo
pinned on her breast, and he plump, jovial, and a specialist at
telling jokes that made nobody laugh. And the house! A turn-
of-the-century little villa in the middle-class part of town, depressing furniture and sofas bestrewn with lace doilies, paper
flowers and old oval photographs on the walls, the whole ge-
nealogy of the family Aunt Pitù was so proud of. And Christmas dinner. A nightmare. Starting with the inevitable cabbage

soup served in the Cantonese porcelain bowls that were Aunt Pitù's pride and joy, and the tenderness with which his mother encouraged him to eat up even though he was gagging over it. And then the torture of being woken up at eleven o'clock at night to attend Low Mass, the ritual of being forced into his best suit, and setting forth into the chill December mists of Oporto. The wintry mists of Oporto. Firmino thought it over and came to the conclusion that his dislike of that city was a hangover from his childhood, maybe Freud was right. He pondered over Freud's theories. Not that he knew them all that well, rather that they didn't inspire enough faith in him. Lukács, on the other hand, with his precise X-ray of literature as an expression of class, he was a different matter, and besides he was useful to his studies of the post-war Portuguese novel. Yes, Lukács was more use to him than Freud, but it could be that that old Viennese doctor was right about certain things, who knows?

"But where is this blessèd boarding-house?" he asked the cabbie.

He felt he had the right to do so. They had been on the road for at least half an hour, at first in the broad thoroughfares of the center and now in the impossibly narrow alleyways of a district unknown to Firmino.

"It takes the time it takes," came the surly mutter of the cabbie.

Taximen and policemen, thought Firmino, were the two types he hated most. And yet in his job most of his dealings were with policemen and taximen. He was a journalist on a periodical specializing in scandals and murder victims, divorces, disemboweled women and beheaded corpses, and that was his life. He thought how wonderful it would be to write his book on Vittorini and the post-war Portuguese novel, he was sure it would be an event in the academic world, and might even lead eventually to a research grant.

The taxi stopped plumb in the middle of a narrow street, before a building that showed every year of its age, and the driver unexpectedly turned towards Firmino and bade him a hearty farewell.

"Afraid you wouldn't get here, eh? young gentleman," he said kindly, "but here in Oporto we don't cheat anyone, we don't go round and round the mulberry bush to rook the customers of their money, we're not in Lisbon here, you know."

Firmino alighted, got out his bag and paid. Above the main door a sign read "Pension Rosa—First Floor." The entrance hall was set up as a ladies' hair salon. There was no elevator. Firmino climbed a staircase embellished with a red banister, or one which had once been red, which saddened him and at the same time made him feel at home. Only too well did he know the sort of boarding-house his Editor habitually sent him to: dreary suppers at seven in the evening, bedrooms with a washbasin in the corner, and worst of all the old harridans who owned them.

But this time it was nothing of the sort, at least as far as the owner was concerned. Dona Rosa, a lady of about sixty, her hair arranged in a blue permanent wave, was not wearing a flower-patterned housecoat like the proprietresses of all the other pensions he had known, but a stylish grey coat and skirt and a jovial smile. Dona Rosa bade him welcome and carefully explained the timetable of the establishment. Dinner was at eight, and that evening it would consist of tripe *à la mode d'Oporto*. If he wished to fend for himself for supper, in the square to the right as he left the house there was a long-established café, the Café Àncora, one of the oldest in Oporto, practically an institution, where the food was good and

reasonably priced, but before that perhaps he had better have
a shower, wouldn't he like to see his room? it was the second
on the right down the corridor, she would appreciate a couple
of words with him but they could have them after dinner, she
was a night owl anyway.

When Firmino entered his room his good first impressions
of the Pension Rosa were confirmed. A spacious window giving on to the garden behind the house, a high ceiling, solid
country furniture, a double bed. A bathroom with flower-
patterned tiles and a bathtub. There was even a hair-dryer.
Firmino undressed without hurry and had a lukewarm shower.
All, in all, here in Oporto there wasn't that sticky heat he had
been afraid of, or at least his room was nice and cool. He put
on a short-sleeved shirt, threw a light jacket over his arm just
in case, and went out. The street outside was still showing
signs of life. The shops were already shuttered up, but folks
were at their windows enjoying the evening air and chatting
with their neighbors across the way. He dawdled a bit to listen
in to this prattle, which he found rather touching. He caught a
few phrases here and there, especially those of a sturdily-built
young lady leaning far out over the sill. She was carrying on
about the Porto football team which had won a match in Germany the day before. She seemed particularly enthusiastic
about the center forward, whose name was unknown to
Firmino.

He spotted the café as soon as he entered the square. He
could scarcely have missed it. It was a nineteenth-century
building with an elaborately stuccoed façade and a heavy
timber-framed doorway. The sign depicted a rubicund little
man sitting astride a barrel of wine. And in Firmino went.

The main room of the café was immense, with its old
wooden tables, its enormous inlaid counter and a host of re-
volving brass fans hanging from the ceiling. The tables right

down the end were reserved for the restaurant, but there were no clients. Firmino took a seat and prepared for a lavish dinner by studying the menu carefully. He made up his mind, and already felt his mouth watering when the waiter arrived. A slender youngster with a little brown beard and a crew-cut.

"The kitchen is closed, sir," said the waiter, "only cold dishes are available."

Firmino glanced at his watch. It was half-past eleven, he had no idea it had got so late. However, in Lisbon you could dine at your leisure at this hour.

"In Lisbon one can still have dinner at this time of night," he said, just for something to say.

"Lisbon is Lisbon and Oporto is Oporto," replied the waiter philosophically, "but I think you will find that our cold dishes will not disappoint you, and if I may make a suggestion, the cook has prepared a shrimp salad with home-made mayonnaise that would make the dead arise."

Firmino said yes to it and the waiter soon returned with the platter of shrimp salad. He served him a generous helping, and said in the meanwhile:

"Porto won yesterday's match in Germany, the German players are tough, but our boys beat them on speed."

Clearly he was in the mood for a chat, and Firmino fell in with this.

"Porto's a fine team," he replied, "but it doesn't have the tradition that Benfica has."

"You're from Lisbon, then?" asked the waiter promptly.

"The center of Lisbon," Firmino assured him.

"I thought so from your accent," said the waiter. "And what brings you here to Oporto?"

"I'm looking for a gypsy," answered Firmino without a thought.

"A gypsy?" asked the waiter.

"Yes, a gypsy," repeated Firmino.

"I'm on the side of the gypsies," said the waiter as if feeling out his ground. "What about you?"

"I don't know much about them," replied Firmino, "in fact very little indeed."

"It may be because I come from Barcelos," said the waiter. "You know, when I was a child in Barcelos they held the grandest fair in the whole of the Minho, but now it's not what it used to be, I went back last year and found it really sad and depressing, but in those days it was a sight to see, but I don't want to bore you, perhaps I'm bothering you?"

"Not at all," said Firmino, "in fact sit down and keep me company, can I offer you a glass of wine?"

The waiter sat down and accepted the glass of wine.

"I was telling you about the fair at Barcelos," the waiter went on, "when I was a child it was magnificent, especially on account of the livestock in the market, those pure-bred Minhota oxen with the long, long horns, do you remember them? but in any case they're a thing of the past, but also the horses, the fillies, the foals, the mares, my father was a horse-dealer and used to do business with the gypsies during the summer months, they had splendid horses, the gypsies did, and were persons worthy of honor and esteem, I remember a banquet they gave my father after concluding some transaction, it was at a big table out in the main square of Barcelos and my father took me along with him."

He paused a while.

"I don't know why I'm pestering you with my memories of childhood," he resumed, "but maybe it's because I feel really sorry for the gypsies today, they're reduced to poverty and what's more everybody is against them."

"Is that the case?" said Firmino, "I didn't know."

"It's a nasty business around these parts," added the waiter, "perhaps I'll tell you about it some other time, I hope you've enjoyed our restaurant and will visit us again."

"The shrimp salad was delicious," Firmino assured him.

He too would have liked to stay on and chat, but he remembered that Dona Rosa wished to have a word with him, so he paid the bill and hurried back to the pension. He found her in the sitting-room reading a magazine. She patted the sofa beside her as an invitation to sit down and he did so. Dona Rosa asked if he had enjoyed his dinner and Firmino said he had, and also that the waiter, a very friendly fellow, was on excellent terms with the gypsies.

"We too are on excellent terms with the gypsies," replied Dona Rosa.

"We who?"

"The Pension Dona Rosa," replied Dona Rosa.

And giving him a broad grin she added: "Manolo the Gypsy is expecting you at midday tomorrow at the encampment, he has agreed to have a talk with you."

Firmino looked at her in astonishment.

"Did you contact him through the police?" he asked.

"Dona Rosa does not use police channels," replied Dona Rosa levelly.

"Then how did you manage it?" persisted Firmino.

"All a good journalist needs is the contact, don't you think?" said Dona Rosa with a wink.

"Where is this encampment?" asked Firmino.

Dona Rosa unfolded a map of the city which she had ready on the table.

"As far as Matosinhos you can go by bus," she explained, "but after that you have to take a taxi, the encampment is just here, you see? Where the green splodge is, it's land belonging to the council. Manolo will be waiting for you at the general store on the edge of the encampment."

Dona Rosa refolded the map implying that that was all she had to tell him, but: "Do you carry a tape recorder?" she asked.

Firmino nodded.

"Keep it in your pocket," said Dona Rosa, "the gypsies don't like tape recorders."

She got up and started switching off the lights, making it plain that it was time for bed. Firmino also got up and was about to take his leave.

"How old are you?" asked Dona Rosa.

Firmino replied with a formula he used whenever he felt too embarrassed to confess that he was only twenty-seven. It was a clumsy formula, but he never managed to find anything better.

"Close on thirty," he said.

"Too young for a filthy job like this," grumbled Dona Rosa. Then she added: "See you tomorrow and, sleep well."

Four

MANOLO THE GYPSY WAS SEATED at a little table under the shop's pergola. He wore a black jacket and a broad-brimmed hat in the Spanish style. His whole air was that of lost nobility: his poverty could be read in every line of his face and in his tattered shirtfront.

Firmino had entered the shop by the front door, which gave on to a pretty little street lined with modest but well-tended villas. But there behind the shop the prospect was quite a different matter. Beyond the sagging chicken-wire that marked the boundary of the shop premises lay the gypsy encampment: six or seven dilapidated caravans, a number of pasteboard shacks, two American cars dating from the 1960s, and half-naked children playing in a dusty clearing. Under a shelter of dry foliage a horse and a donkey were swishing their tails to keep the flies away.

"Good morning," said Firmino, "my name is Firmino." And he held out his hand.

Manolo touched his cap with two fingers and shook hands.

"Thank you for agreeing to meet me," said Firmino.

Manolo made no reply, but pulled out his pipe and crumbled two yellowed cigarettes into the bowl. His face betrayed nothing whatever and his gaze was directed upwards at the pergola.

Firmino put his notepad and pen on the table.

"May I take notes?" he asked.

Manolo gave no answer and continued to survey the pergola.

Then he said: "How many *baguines*?"

"*Baguines*?" queried Firmino.

At last Manolo looked at him. He seemed annoyed.

"*Baguines, parné*. Don't you understand *geringonça*?"

It occurred to Firmino that things were not taking the right turn. He felt a fool, and more of a fool still when he thought of the little Sony in his pocket that had cost him the earth.

"I also speak Portuguese, but I prefer *geringonça*," explained Manolo.

Well, the truth was that Firmino was not able to understand the gypsy dialect, what Manolo called *geringonça*. He made an effort to solve the problem by finding a logical thread, beginning at the beginning.

"May I write your name?"

"Manolo El Rey does not end up in the *cagarrão*," answered Manolo, crossing his wrists and then putting a finger to his lips. Firmino gathered that the *cagarrão* must mean prison or at least the police.

"Very well," he said, "no names, and now please repeat your request."

"How many *baguines*?" repeated Manolo, rubbing his thumb and forefinger together as if counting money.

Firmino made a rapid calculation. For immediate expenses the Editor had given him forty thousand escudos. Ten thousand might be the right price for Manolo, after all he had agreed to talk to him, which was already extraordinary for a gypsy, and maybe he'd be able to worm something out of him that he hadn't told the police. But what if Manolo knew nothing more than he had already said, and this appointment was just a trick to get his hands on a few *baguines*, as he would put it? Firmino tried to play for time.

"It depends on what you tell me," he said, "whether what you have to say is worth my while."

"How many *baguines*?" and again the rubbing of forefinger and thumb.

Take it or leave it, thought Firmino, there was nothing else for it.

"Ten thousand escudos," he said, "no more and no less."

Manolo gave an imperceptible nod of acceptance.

"A *chavelho*," he murmured. And he brought his thumb to his mouth, tipping his head back.

This time Firmino had no trouble in getting the message, so he went into the shop and returned with a liter of red wine. On the way he slipped a hand into his pocket and turned off the tape recorder. He couldn't say why he did it. Perhaps because he had taken a liking to Manolo at first sight. He liked the expression on his face, stony and at the same time bewildered, in a way even desperate, and the voice of that old gypsy deserved a better fate than to be filched by some Japanese electronic gadget.

"Tell me everything," said Firmino, and put his elbows on the table with his fists against his temples as he did when he wanted to concentrate. He could even do without his notebook, his memory would suffice.

Manolo approached the matter in a roundabout way. On the whole he explained himself pretty well, and as for the words in *geringonça*, Firmino could not decode them but managed to guess at the meaning by following the thread. The gypsy began by saying that he had trouble sleeping, that he often woke in the middle of the night because that's the way it is with old people, because they wake up and think back over their whole lives, and this distresses them, because thinking of one's past life is a source of regret, especially for those of the gypsy people, who at one time were noble but have now become beggars but he was old only in his mind and spirit, not in his body, because he still retained his virility, it was only that with his wife his virility was useless because she was an old woman, and so he got up and went to empty his bladder in order to relieve himself. And he went on to speak of Manolito, who was his son's son, and said he had blue eyes and a sad future to look forward to, because what future could there be in a world like this for a gypsy boy? Then he began to go off at a tangent and asked Firmino if he knew a place called Janas. Firmino listened attentively. He liked the way Manolo talked, with those rounded periods sprinkled with words in dialect, so he asked with genuine interest: "Where is Janas?"

Manolo explained that it was not far inland from Lisbon, in the vicinity of Mafra, where there was an ancient circular chapel dating from early Christian times during the Roman Empire, and that this place was sacred to the gypsies, because the gypsies have roamed the Iberian peninsula since very ancient times, and every year, on the fifteenth of August, the gypsies of Portugal used to gather at Janas for a great festival of singing and dancing, the guitars and accordions were never silent for a moment and the meals were prepared on great braziers at the foot of the hill, and then, at sunset, at the very moment the sun touched the horizon, when its rays reddened the whole plain down as far as the cliffs of Ericeira, the priest who had celebrated Mass would come out of the chapel to bless the gypsies' livestock, the mules and the horses, the finest horses in the whole Iberian peninsula, which the gypsies then sold to the stables at Alter do Chão, where they were trained for the bullfights, but now, now that the gypsies no longer had horses but bought horrible motor cars what was there to bless? Could one bless a motor car, which is made of metal? Certainly with horses if you don't give them hay and oats they die, whereas with cars, if you haven't the money to put petrol in them they don't die, and when you do put petrol in off they go again, and this was why those gypsies who had a bit of money bought cars, but what point would there be in blessing a motor car?

Manolo gave him a questioning look, as if expecting him to come up with a solution, and the old man's face wore an expression of profound unhappiness.

Firmino lowered his eyes, almost as if he were personally responsible for what was happening to Manolo's people, and he lacked the courage to urge him to go on. But Manolo continued without urging, including details that he probably considered of interest, about how he was pissing against the great oak when he had spotted the shoe protruding from the bushes. Then centimeter by centimeter he described what he had seen as he examined the body, and said that on the corpse's T-shirt there were words in a foreign language, which he spelt out because he didn't know how to pronounce them, and Firmino wrote them down on his notepad.

"Like this?" asked Firmino, "was it written like this?"

Manolo confirmed that that was it: Stones of Portugal.

"But the police have stated that the body was naked from the waist up," objected Firmino, "the newspapers say that it was naked from the waist up."

"No," confirmed Manolo, "there were these words, these very words."

"Go on," said Firmino.

Manolo did so, but the rest of it Firmino already knew. It was what Manolo had told the shopkeeper and subsequently confirmed to the police. Firmino doubted he could gain anything more from the old gypsy, but something told him to press on.

"You sleep badly Manolo," he said, "did you hear anything that night?"

Manolo held out his glass and Firmino refilled it. The gypsy knocked back the wine and murmured: "Manolo drinks, but his people are in need of *alcide*."

"What is *alcide*?" asked Firmino.

Manolo consented to translate: "Bread."

"Did you hear anything during the night?" repeated Firmino.

"An engine," said Manolo promptly.

"Do you mean a car?" asked Firmino.

"A car and car doors slamming."

"Where?"

"Near my hut."

"Can a car get all the way to your hut?"

Manolo pointed to a dirt track that ran at an angle off the main road and along the edge of the encampment.

"On that track you can reach the big oak and go on down the hill all the way to the river."

"Did you hear voices?"

"Yes, voices," said Manolo.

"What did they say?"

"I don't know, impossible to understand."

"Not even a word?" insisted Firmino.

"One word," said Manolo, "I heard someone say *cagarrão*."

"Prison?" asked Firmino.

"Yes, prison," confirmed Manolo.

"What happened then?"

"I don't know," said Manolo, "but one of them had a great *gateira*."

"What does *gateira* mean?" asked Firmino.

Manolo pointed to the bottle of wine.

"He had been drinking," said Firmino, "is that what you mean, that he was drunk?"

Manolo nodded.

"How did you realize that?"

"He laughed like someone who is very drunk."

"Did you hear anything else?"

Manolo shook his head.

"Think well," Manolo, said Firmino, "because anything you can remember is very important to me."

Manolo appeared to be thinking hard.

"How many of them do you think there were?" asked Firmino.

"Two or maybe three," replied Manolo, "I can't be sure."

"Don't you remember anything else that might be important?"

Manolo gave himself up to reflection and drank another glass of wine. The shopkeeper came to the back door and lounged there eyeing them with curiosity.

"Shittipants is what we call him," said Manolo, "I owe him two thousand escudos for aqua vitae."

"You'll be able to pay him off with the money you'll get from me," Firmino reassured him.

"One of them spoke badly," said Manolo.

"How do you mean?" asked Firmino.

"He spoke badly."

"Do you mean he didn't speak Portuguese?"

"No," said Manolo, "he spoke like this: G-G-G-God d-dammit, G-G-G-God d-dammit."

"I see," said Firmino, "he stammered."

"That's it," agreed Manolo.

"Is there anything else?" asked Firmino.

Manolo shook his head.

Firmino pulled out his wallet and handed over ten thousand escudos. They vanished into Manolo's pocket with astonishing speed. Firmino got to his feet and held out his hand. Manolo shook it and touched his cap with two fingers.

"Go to Janas," said Manolo, "it's a fine place."

"I'll go, sooner or later," promised Firmino while leaving. He went into the shop and asked the proprietor to call him a cab.

"Waste of time," said the shopkeeper rudely, "cabs won't come all the way out here for a phone-call."

"I've got to get to town," said Firmino.

The shopkeeper swatted away the flies with a dirty rag and said there was a bus.

"Where is the bus stop?"

"A kilometer away if you bear left."

Firmino went out into the scorching sunlight. Damn you, Shittipants, he thought. The heat was ferocious, that real humid heat that typifies Oporto. No one went by on the road, he couldn't even thumb a lift. He thought that as soon as he got back to the Pension Rosa he would write the article and fax it off to the paper. It would be out in two days. He could already see the headline: THE MAN WHO FOUND THE HEADLESS CORPSE TELLS ALL. And immediately beneath: From Our Special Correspondent in Oporto. The entire story from beginning to end, just as Manolo had told it, including that mysterious car that stopped near his hut in the middle of the night. And the voices in the dark. Crimes and mysteries such the readers of his paper wanted. But the fact that one of those unknown voices had a stammer he would not say. Firmino did not know why, but he would keep this detail to himself, he wouldn't reveal it to his readers.

At a wider curve in the deserted road an enormous billboard for TAP Air Portugal, depicting a cobalt-blue sea, promised him a Dream Holiday in Madeira.

Five

"HELL AND DAMMIT," said Firmino, "how can I say I dislike a town when I don't even know it? The thing's illogical, it shows a real lack of proper dialectics. Lukács held that direct knowledge of the facts is the indispensable instrument for forming a critical opinion. No doubt about it."

So he went into a big bookshop and sought a guidebook. His choice fell on a recent publication with a handsome blue cover and splendid colored photographs. The author's name was Helder Pacheco, who apart from showing a high degree of competence also revealed a boundless love for the city of Oporto. Firmino detested those technical, impersonal, objective guidebooks that dish up information stone cold. He went for things done with enthusiasm, not least because he really needed enthusiasm in the position in which he found himself.

Armed with this book he began to walk about the city hunting happily in the guidebook for the places where his random footsteps led him. He found himself in Rua S. Bento da Vitória and at once took a liking to the spot, chiefly because even on such a scorching day it was a dark, cool street, where the sun seemed never to penetrate. He looked it up in the index, which was easy to consult, and found it straightaway on page 132. He discovered that it had once been called Rua S. Miguel, and that in 1600 a monk called Pereira de Novais, of whom he had never heard, had written a picturesque account of it in Spanish. He relished the monk's pompous descriptions of the "*casas hermosas de algunos hidalgos,*" ministers, chancellors and other notables of the city now lost in the mists of time, but whose lives were attested to by architectural evidence: pediments and capitals in the Ionic style, recalling the noble and sumptuous days of that thoroughfare, before the inclemencies of history transformed it into the working-class street it was today. He pushed on with his inspection and arrived at a rather impressive mansion. The guidebook told him that it had once belonged to the Baroness da Regaleira, had been built at the end of the eighteenth century by one José Monteiro de Almeida, a Portuguese merchant in London, and had served in succession as the central post office, a Carmelite convent, and a state lycée, until being turned to its present use as the headquarters of the police crime squad. Firmino paused for a moment before its majestic doorway. The crime squad. Who knows if someone in there was not following the uncertain track of the headless corpse, as he was himself. Who knows if some austere magistrate, immersed in deciphering the reports of the forensic experts who had carried out the autopsy, was not even now attempting to put an identity to that mutilated body.

Firmino glanced at his watch and walked on. It was nearly midday. *Acontecimento* should be on the newsstands of Oporto by now, it arrived by the morning flight. He came into a square which he didn't bother to look up in the guidebook. He made for a kiosk and bought the paper. He sat on a bench. *Acontecimento* gave the whole front page to it, with an illustration in violet ink showing the silhouette of a headless body and above it a knife dripping with blood. The headline read: STILL NO NAME FOR HEADLESS CORPSE. His article was on the inside pages. Firmino read it carefully through and

saw that there were no substantial changes. He noticed, however, that his description of the blue T-shirt had been tinkered
with, and this riled him. He made for a telephone booth and
called the paper. He was answered, of course, by Senhora
Odette, who started nattering away at once, poor thing, sitting
there in her wheelchair, the telephone was her only contact
with the world. She wanted to know if they ate as much tripe
in Oporto as people said they did, and Firmino replied that so
far he had managed to avoid it. Then she asked if it was more
beautiful than Lisbon, and Firmino replied that it was different, but had its charm which he was in the process of discover-
ing. Finally she congratulated him on his article, which she
had found "gripping," and gave him to understand how lucky
he was in life to have such exciting adventures. At long last she
put him through to the Editor.

"Hullo," said Firmino, "I see that you are being cagey."

The Editor chuckled. "It's a question of strategy," he said.

"I don't see the point," said Firmino.

"Listen here Firmino," explained the Editor, "you claim
that Manolo the Gypsy gave the police an exact description of
the T-shirt, but in their official communiqué the police have
said that the body was naked from the waist up."

"Exactly," said Firmino impatiently, "and so?"

"And so there must be a reason," insisted the Editor, "and
we won't be the ones to contradict the police. I think it better
for us to say that we've heard rumors that the corpse was wearing a T-shirt printed with the words Stones of Portugal, imagine if Manolo invented the whole thing."

"But we'll lose the scoop if we don't say that the police kept
quiet about the T-shirt," protested Firmino.

"There must be a reason for that," repeated the Editor,
"and it would be great if you managed to find out."

Firmino could scarcely hold his tongue. What grandiose

notions came into the Editor's head! The police wouldn't even receive him, imagine them answering questions from a journalist.

"And what the hell would you do?" asked Firmino.

"Rack your brains," said the Editor, "you're young and have plenty of imagination."

"Who is the examining magistrate on the case?" asked Firmino.

"Dr. Quartim, as you know, but you won't get a thing from him because all his information comes from the police."

"It looks like a real vicious circle," commented Firmino.

"Rack your brains," repeated the Editor, "it's precisely to find out these things that I've sent you to Oporto."

Firmino left the booth streaming with sweat. Now he felt more irritable than ever. He made for the little fountain in the square and bathed his face. "Damn it," he thought, "what next?" There was a bus stop at the corner. Firmino managed to jump aboard a bus that took him into the center of town. He was rather pleased with himself because he now knew the chief landmarks in a city which had at first seemed hostile. He asked the driver to drop him off when they came to some shopping center. At the driver's signal he got off, and only then realized that he had not even paid his fare. He entered the shopping center, a colossal area which some intelligent architect, a rare species nowadays, had created out of many old buildings without ruining their façades. Oporto was a well-organized city: in the entrance, a spacious foyer with numerous escalators leading to the basement or to the upper floors, was a counter from behind which a pretty girl in blue was distributing leaflets indicating all the shops in the center and exactly where to find them. Firmino studied this leaflet and set off resolutely for corridor B on the first floor. The shop was called "T-shirt International." It was full of mirrors and had cubicles for changing and shelves overflowing with goods. Several youths were there trying on T-shirts and checking themselves out in the mirror. Firmino applied to the assistant, a girl with long fair hair.

"I'd like a T-shirt," he said, "a particular T-shirt."

"We cater for all tastes sir," replied the girl.

"Made in Portugal?" asked Firmino.

"Both here and abroad," replied the girl, "we import from France, Italy, England and especially the United States."

"Fine," said Firmino, "the color is probably blue, but it might come in other colors, the important thing is the words on it."

"What are they?" she asked.

"Stones of Portugal," said Firmino.

The girl looked thoughtful for a moment. She twisted her mouth slightly as if the words meant nothing to her, opened a large typewritten catalogue and ran her index finger down the lists of names.

"I'm sorry sir," she said, "we don't carry that line."

"All the same," said Firmino, "I've seen it, I passed a chap in the street who was wearing one."

The girl did some more thinking.

"Perhaps it's an advertisement," she suggested, "we don't carry publicity T-shirts, only ones on the open market."

Firmino did some thinking too. Publicity. Maybe it was a publicity stunt.

"Yes," he said, "but an advertisement for what, what do you think Stones of Portugal could mean?"

"Well," said the girl, "it could be a new rock group that's given a concert, when there's a concert they usually sell advertising T-shirts at the entrance, why not try a record shop? They sell T-shirts along with the records."

Firmino said thank you and looked in the leaflet for the record shop. Classical music or modern music? Naturally he opted for modern music. It was in the same corridor. The youth at the counter had a headset on and was listening in an enraptured way. Firmino waited patiently until he came out of his trance.

"Do you know a group called Stones of Portugal?" he asked.

The assistant looked at him and assumed a thoughtful air. "I don't think so," he replied, "is it a new group?"

"Could be," said Firmino.

"Very new?"

"Could be."

"We're pretty up to date with new events," the youth assured him, "and the most recent groups are the Novos Ricos and the Lisbon Ravens, but the group you mention frankly doesn't ring a bell, though it could be an amateur group, of course."

"Do you think an amateur group would be able to produce publicity T-shirts?" asked Firmino, fast losing hope.

"Not on your life," replied the assistant, "most times even the pro's can't afford it, we live in Portugal you know, not in the United States."

Firmino thanked him and left. It was nearly two in the afternoon. He wasn't in the mood to look for a restaurant. Maybe he'd find a bite to eat at Dona Rosa's. Just as long as the *plat du jour* wasn't tripe.

Six

No, Dona Rosa's *plat du jour* that day was *rojoes à la mode de Minho*. Perhaps it was not a dish particularly suited to the heat of Oporto, but Firmino was crazy about those hunks of pork fillet sautéed with potatoes.

There he was in the dining-room for the first time since his arrival at the pension. Three tables were occupied. Dona Rosa came in and wanted to introduce him to the other guests, she was determined on it. Firmino followed. The first, one Senhor Paulo, was a man of about fifty, who imported meat into the Setabal district. He was bald and robust. The second, Signor Bianchi, was an Italian who spoke no Portuguese but expressed himself in halting French. He owned a firm which bought boletus mushrooms, both fresh and dried, for export to Italy, because the Portuguese cared very little about mushrooms. He declared with a smile that trade was flourishing and that he hoped that the Portuguese would continue to care very little about boletus mushrooms. Finally there was a couple from Aveiro who were celebrating their silver wedding anniversary and making a second honeymoon of it. Firmino wondered why they had chosen this pension.

Dona Rosa then told him that the Editor had been trying to reach him and wanted him to call back urgently. Firmino decided to keep the Editor waiting for a while, otherwise all those goodies doing the rounds of the table would get cold. He ate slowly and with relish, because the pork was absolutely exquisite. He ordered coffee and only when he had drunk it did he resign himself to calling up the paper.

The telephone was in the lounge, for the bedrooms only had house phones connected with the reception desk. Firmino put in his money and dialed. The Editor was out. Senhora Odette put him through to Senhor Silva, whom Firmino immediately called Huppert, to put him in a good mood. Silva was solicitous and paternal.

"We've had an anonymous call," he said, "he won't talk to us, he wants to talk directly to the special correspondent, which is you, we've given him the number of the pension and he's going to ring at four o'clock, in my opinion he was calling from Oporto."

Silva paused.

"Are you enjoying your nice trip?" he asked perfidiously.

Firmino replied that he had just finished eating a dish that he, Silva, could not have imagined in his wildest dreams.

"Don't leave the pension," entreated Silva, "it could be a mythomaniac, but he didn't give me that impression, treat him well, he may have important information for you."

Firmino glanced at his watch and took a seat on the sofa. Dammit, he thought, now even that ass Silva took the liberty of giving him advice. He picked a magazine out of a wicker basket. It was called *Vultos*, and was devoted to the Portuguese and international jet-set. He settled down to read with interest an article about the claimant to the throne of Portugal, Don Duarte de Braganca, who had just become the father of a son. The claimant, wearing a mustache in the nineteenth-century manner, was sitting bolt upright in a high-backed leather chair and holding the hand of his consort, who was buried so deep in a low chair that only her shins and neck were visible, as if she had been sawn in half. Firmino concluded that the photographer was totally incompetent, but he had no time to finish the article because the telephone rang. He waited for Dona Rosa to answer it.

"It's for you, Senhor Firmino," said Dona Rosa amiably.

"Hullo," said Firmino into the instrument.

"Look in the yellow pages," murmured the voice at the other end of the wire.

"Look for what?" asked Firmino.

"For Stones of Portugal," said the voice, "under Import-Export."

"Who are you?" asked Firmino.

"It doesn't matter," answered the voice.

"Why don't you telephone the police instead of me?" inquired Firmino.

"Because I know the police better than you do," replied the voice. And the line went dead.

Firmino set himself to thinking. It was a young voice with a strong Northern accent. Not an educated person, that was plain from his pronunciation. And so? And so what? The North of Portugal was full of uneducated young men with strong Northern accents. He picked up the telephone directory from the little table and looked through the Yellow Pages for the section Import-Export. It said: Stones of Portugal, Vila Nova de Gaia, Avenida Heróis do Mar, 123. He looked in his guidebook but it wasn't any help to him. There was nothing to do but ask Dona Rosa. Dona Rosa very patiently unfolded the map of Oporto once more and showed him the place. It certainly wasn't just round the corner, it was right on the other side of town and practically not in Oporto at all. In fact Vila Nova was a town of its own, with a town hall and everything else. He was in a hurry? Well in that case the only thing was to take a taxi, because by public transport he wouldn't get there until dinner-time, and how much a taxi would cost him she simply couldn't say, she'd never been to Vila Nova by taxi, but of course luxuries have to be paid for.

"And now goodbye young man," she said, she was going to have a short siesta, yes, that's just what she needed.

AVENIDA HERÓIS DO MAR was a long street on the outskirts lined with a few stunted trees and small building sites, half-finished buildings, warehouses and brand-new little villas with gardens full of effigies of Snow White and ceramic swallows on the walls of the verandas. Number 123 was a white, single-story building with an undulating wall in the Mexican style. In its rear rose a large warehouse with a corrugated-iron roof. On the wall a brass plaque read: Stones of Portugal. Firmino pressed the electronic button and the gate clicked open. The building itself had a little portico along the front, like the other villas in the street, and on one of the columns was a sign saying "Administration." Firmino went in. It was a little office equipped with modern furniture, but not devoid of good taste. At a glass-topped table cluttered with documents sat an elderly, bald, bespectacled gentleman tapping away at a typewriter.

"Good afternoon," said Firmino.

The old chap stopped typing and looked up. He returned the greeting.

"The reason for your visit?" he asked.

Firmino felt caught unprepared. He had really been an idiot, he thought, because all through the long taxi-ride he had thought about Manolo, and then his fiancée whom he was already missing, and thereafter how Lukács would have reacted if instead of being confronted by a text of Balzac's he had had to face the naked reality of things, as he himself was doing at the moment. He had thought of all this, but had neglected to think of how he should explain his presence.

"I was looking for the boss," he mumbled.

"The boss is in Hong Kong," said the old boy, "he'll be away till the end of the month."

"Who can I talk to then?" asked Firmino.

"The secretary has taken a week's holiday," was the answer, "so there's just the warehouseman and me, I'm responsible for the accounting, is it a matter of urgency?"

"Yes and no," replied Firmino, "but as I'm passing through Oporto I wanted to make a proposal to your boss."

Then, as if to make his presence a little more convincing, he added: "I'm in the business myself, I have a small firm in Lisbon."

"Ah," replied the employee without the least vestige of interest.

"May I sit down for a moment?" asked Firmino.

The man waved a hand at the chair facing the desk. It was a buff-colored canvas chair with arms to it, such as film directors use. It struck Firmino again that whoever had furnished Stones of Portugal had pretty good taste.

"What is your exact line of business?" he enquired with the most charming smile at his disposal.

The old man at last raised his eyes from the papers on his desk. He lit a Gauloise from a packet on the table beside him and inhaled an avid puff.

"Curse it," he said, "these Chinese accounts are hell on earth, they send their statements in Hong Kong dollars and I have to turn them into Portuguese escudos, and the hitch is that the Hong Kong dollar never fluctuates a red cent one way or the other whereas our currency goes up and down like a yo-yo, I don't know whether you follow the Lisbon stock exchange."

Firmino nodded and spread his arms as if to say: ah yes, I know it only too well.

"We began with marble," said the old man, "seven years ago it was just the boss and me, an Alsatian dog and a tin shack."

"Ah yes," said Firmino to urge him to further confidences, "marble really goes, here in this country."

"*If* it goes," returned the old man, "*if* it goes. But you have to find the right market. The boss has an extraordinary flair for these things, maybe he's had a bit of luck as well, but I can't deny he's got a real business sense, and that's why he thought of Italy."

Firmino's face took on an expression of wonderment.

"It seems to me a pretty queer notion, exporting marble to Italy," he said, "the Italians are up to their eyeballs in marble."

"So you think, my dear sir," exclaimed the old man, "and so I thought myself, but this means that we don't have a flair for these things and don't know the laws of the market. I'll say one thing: do you know which is the most highly prized marble in Italy? That's easy enough, it's the marble from Carrara. And what does the Italian market demand? Easy again: marble from Carrara. But it so happens that Carrara is no longer able to satisfy the demands, my dear sir, I don't know the exact reasons, let's say because labor is too expensive, the quarrymen are anarchists and have very demanding trade unions, that the environmentalists are making life hell for the government because the Apuan Alps have been riddled with holes, things of that sort."

The old fellow drew greedily at his cigarette.

"Well then my dear sir," he resumed, "do you by any chance know anything about the marble of Estremoz?"

Firmino gave a vague nod.

"Same characteristics as Carrara marble," said the old man complacently, "same porosity, same veining, same reaction to machine polishing, the same in every way as Carrara marble."

And the old man heaved a sigh as if he had revealed the secret of the century.

"Do I make myself clear?" he asked.

"Perfectly," said Firmino.

"Please explain," said Firmino.

"Good," continued the old man, "it's like Columbus's egg. The boss sends Estremoz marble to Carrara and they resell it on the Italian market as Carrara marble, and so there you have the atriums of Roman apartment houses and the bathrooms of wealthy Italians tiled with fine Carrara marble which comes from Estremoz in Portugal. And it's not that the boss has to do the thing on a vast scale, you know, he has simply subleased a firm in Estremoz which cuts the blocks and ships them from Setúbal. However, with the cost of labor in Portugal being as low as it is, do you realize what that means to us?"

He waited with an air of impatience for Firmino's answer, which never came.

"Millions," he said in answer to his own question, and then went on: "And as one thing leads to another the boss started looking for another market, and he found Hong Kong, because the Chinese also are mad for Carrara marble, and since a thing that leads to another leads to another again, the boss thought that since we were in the export business the moment had come to import as well, so we became an import-export firm, it doesn't show on the surface, we have these modest premises, but that's only so as not to flaunt the fact that we have one of the biggest annual turnovers of any firm in Oporto, you who are in business can understand that the financial police have to be kept at arm's length, but you know my boss has two Ferrari Testarossas, he keeps them out at his farm in the country, and d'you know what he did before this?"

"I have no idea," replied Firmino.

"Worked for the Council," said the old man with great

satisfaction, "in the stewarts' office, at the Town that means having a flair for business, of course he's had to play at politics a bit, it's only logical, without politics you can't get anywhere in this country, so he got himself made election campaign manager of the aspiring candidate for the mayorship of his town, took him by car to every political meeting in the province of Minho, the mayor was elected and as a reward gave him this piece of land for thruppence and arranged for the license to start up the business. Speaking of which, what exact line is your firm into?"

"Clothing," replied Firmino craftily enough.

The old man lit another Gauloise.

"And so?" he asked.

"We're opening a chain of shops in Algarve," said Firmino, "mostly jeans and T-shirts, because Algarve is a place for young people, all beaches and discotheques, and we've decided to market the most bizarre T-shirts, because the kids nowadays want them as bizarre as you please, if you try and sell a T-shirt saying Harvard University no one would buy it, but with T-shirts like yours maybe they would, and we could mass-produce them."

The old man got up, made his way to a closet with a folding door, rummaged around in a big box.

"Is this what you mean?"

It was a blue T-shirt bearing the words Stones of Portugal. The very thing described by Manolo.

The accountant gave him a look and then handed it to him.

"By all means take it," he said, "but have a word with the secretary about it next week, I can't tell you anything."

"What is it you import?" asked Firmino.

"High technology instruments from Hong Kong," replied

the old man, "equipment for hi-fi and for hospitals, and that's the reason I'm in trouble."

"Why is that?" asked Firmino in the most tactful of tones.

"We had a robbery five days ago," came the answer, "it was during the night, they disconnected the alarm system and made straight for the container with the equipment in it as if they knew exactly where to look, and they only stole two highly sophisticated components for CAT machinery, do you know what the CAT is?"

"Computerized axial tomography," answered Firmino.

"Our guard dog," continued the old man "the Alsatian, didn't notice a thing, and the thieves certainly didn't drug him."

"They'd have some trouble selling components for CAT," objected Firmino.

"You'd be surprised," said the old man, "what with all the private clinics springing up in Portugal like mushrooms, forgive me but do you know anything about our health services?"

"Vaguely," said Firmino.

"It's sheer piracy," said the old man with conviction, "that's why medical equipment is so expensive, but the fact is this theft was really odd, as odd as could be. Just imagine, two electronic switches for CAT machines smoothly removed from our containers and abandoned on the roadside only half a kilometer away."

"Abandoned?"

"As if they'd been chucked out of a car window, but reduced to pulp, as if a car had run over them."

"Have you notified the police?" asked Firmino.

"Of course," said the accountant, "because though it's a matter of two tiny little components, they're worth a lot of money."

"Really?" said Firmino

"And what's more with the boss in Hong Kong and the secretary on holiday," grumbled the old boy with some exasperation, "the whole thing falls on my shoulders, even the errand-boy seems to have fallen ill."

"What errand-boy?" asked Firmino.

"The errand-boy who make deliveries," replied the old man, "at least I had an underling to send off on errands, but he hasn't come to work for five days."

"A young fellow?" asked Firmino.

"That's right," confirmed the old man, "a temporary, he came here a couple of months ago looking for work and the boss took him on as an errand-boy."

Firmino had a sudden mental short circuit.

"What's his name?" he asked.

"What's that to you?" the old man asked.

In his eyes there was a hint of suspicion.

"Oh, just a question, it isn't important," said Firmino in an attempt to pass it off.

"Well, he likes to be called Dakota," said the old man, "because he's mad about anything and everything American, and I've always called him Dakota, but I don't know his real name, in fact it doesn't even appear in the register, as I said he's a temporary. Excuse me asking, but why are you so keen to know?"

"No particular reason," replied Firmino, "just a question."

"Very well then," concluded the old man, "now you must forgive me but I have to get back to these accounts, this evening I have to get off a fax to Hong Kong, it's an urgent invoice, if you want further information come back in a week's time, I can't guarantee that the boss will be here but the secretary will have definitely come back."

Seven

"HULLO, EDITOR?" said Firmino, "I'm on the trail, I think I've found the right track. I've traced the corpse's T-shirt, it comes from an import-export firm in Vila Nova de Gaia, they make T-shirts identical to the one Manolo described to me."

"Anything else?" asked the Editor impassably.

"They had an errand-boy," replied Firmino, "a young chap, and he hasn't turned up for work for the last five days. However, I didn't manage to find out his name. Shall we print this?"

"Anything else?" insisted the Editor.

"The firm was burgled five days ago, the thieves got away with two high-tech instruments which they then abandoned at the roadside and squashed under the wheels of their car. The firm is Stones of Portugal, import-export, shall we print this?"

There was a brief silence and then the Editor said: "Take it easy. Let's wait."

"But this looks like a real scoop," exclaimed Firmino.

"Consult with Dona Rosa," ordered the Editor.

"Excuse my asking sir," said Firmino, "but how come that Dona Rosa is so well informed?"

"Dona Rosa knows the kind of people who can be of use to us," explained the Editor, "and in fact in a certain sense she's the queen of Oporto."

"Sorry, but in what sense?" asked Firmino.

"Doesn't she strike you as a pretty classy woman?" insisted the Editor.

"Too much so for a pension like this," replied Firmino.

"Have you ever heard of the Bachus?" asked the Editor.

Firmino said nothing.

"In the old days," said the Editor, "the Bachus was a legendary bar, frequented by everyone who mattered in Oporto, and even those who didn't. And late at night, when being stewed to the gills tends to make people sorry for themselves, everyone to some extent had a good cry on the shoulder of the owner. Who was Dona Rosa."

"And she ended up in this place?" exclaimed Firmino.

"Look here Firmino," burst out the Editor, "just keep calm and don't make such a pest of yourself, stick in there for the moment and see how things work out."

"Yes," said Firmino, "but it's Saturday, and this evening I could catch a train and spend Sunday and Monday morning in Lisbon, don't you think?"

"Forgive me asking, young man, but what would you be doing in Lisbon on Sunday and on Monday morning?"

"That seems obvious," replied Firmino heatedly. "Sunday I'll spend with my fiancée because I think I have a right to, and on Monday morning I'll go to the National Library."

The Editor's voice took on a tone of slight irritation.

"Well I'll accept the excuse of your fiancée, we've all of us had a romantic phase in our lives, but just tell me what you'd be doing on Monday morning at the National Library?"

Firmino braced himself to give a plausible explanation. He well knew that with his Editor you needed tact.

"In the manuscript section there's a letter from Elio Vittorini to a Portuguese writer," he said, "I was told so by Dr. Luis Braz Ferreira."

The Editor was silent for a moment then coughed briefly into the mouthpiece.

"And who might this Dr. Luis Braz Ferreira be?"

"He's a leading expert in manuscripts at the National Library," replied Firmino.

"Hard cheese," said the Editor in contemptuous tones.

"What's that supposed to mean?," asked Firmino, dumbfounded.

"That it's his bad luck, his business" repeated the Editor.

"Excuse me, sir," insisted Firmino, forcing himself to be polite, "but Dr. Braz Ferreira knows every twentieth-century manuscript in the National Library."

"Does he know any headless bodies?" asked the Editor.

"They're not in his field," said Firmino.

"That's his bad luck," concluded the Editor, "I am interested in headless bodies, and at this moment so are you."

"Yes," agreed Firmino, "I see that, but you must realize that the letter in question refers to the books of the 'Três Abelhas' and, whether it interests you or not, these books were absolutely essential to Portuguese culture in the later 1950s, because they published Americans and they all came through Vittorini, on account of an anthology he had published in Italy, called *Americana.*"

"Listen young man," broke in the Editor, "you work for *Acontecimento*, which means me, and *Acontecimento* pays your wages. And I want you to stay in Oporto, and above all stay in Dona Rosa's pension. Don't go for too many walks and don't think about the big picture, as for literature, you can devote yourself to it when you get the chance, but for the moment just sit on the sofa and tell jokes to Dona Rosa, and especially listen to hers, they're some of the best and very clean, so goodbye for now."

The receiver went click and Firmino cast a disconsolate

look at Dona Rosa, who was coming through from the dining-room.

"Why such a gloomy face, young man?" Dona Rosa smiled at him as if she had overheard every word, "don't take it to heart, that's the way bosses are, arrogant. I've met a lot of overbearing people in the course of my life but one must grin and bear it, one of these days we'll sit here and I'll tell you how to deal with overbearing people, but the great thing is to do a good job of work." Then in motherly fashion she added: "Why don't you go and have a nap? You've got bags under your eyes, your room is cool and the sheets are spotless, I have them changed every three days."

Firmino went to his room. He fell into a lovely sleep as he had hoped to and dreamt about a beach in Madeira, a blue blue sea, and his fiancée. When he woke it was time for dinner, so he put on a jacket and went downstairs. He was lucky enough to find that dinner that evening was a favorite childhood dish, fried hake. He ate ravenously, waited on hand and foot by the young waitress, a hefty lass with a pronounced mustache. The Italian at the next table tried to start a conversation about cuisine, and described a dish of sweet peppers and anchovies which he said came from Piedmont. Firmino courteously pretended to be interested. At that moment Dona Rosa approached him and bent down to whisper in his ear.

"The head has been found," she said sweetly.

Firmino was looking at the heads of the hake which were left on his plate.

"Head," he asked like an idiot, "what head?"

"The head missing·from the corpse," said Dona Rosa amiably, "but there's no hurry, first finish eating your dinner, then I'll tell you all about it and what to do. I'll expect you in the lounge."

Firmino was unable to restrain his impatience and rushed after her.

"It was found by Senhor Diocleciano," said Dona Rosa calmly, "he fished it out of the Douro, so now sit down and listen carefully, come and sit by me."

And she gave two little taps on the sofa as usual, as if inviting him to have a cup of tea.

"My friend Diocleciano is eighty years old," Dona Rosa went on, "he's been a peddler, a boatman, and he is a fisherman of corpses and suicides in the Douro. Rumor has it that in his life he has fished over seven hundred bodies out of the river. He hands the bodies over to the morgue and the morgue pays him a wage. It's his job. However, this case he knew about in advance, so he has not yet turned the head over to the authorities. He is also the guardian of souls in the Arco dal Alminhas, in the sense that he concerns himself not simply with bodies but also their eternal repose, he lights candles in that holy place, says prayers for them and so on. He has the head at home, he pulled it out of the river a couple of hours ago and let me know, here's his address. But on your way back don't forget to call in at the Arco das Alminhas and say a prayer for the dead. Meanwhile don't forget to take your camera, before the head ends up in the morgue."

Firmino went up to his room, fetched his camera and went out in search of a taxi, giving no thought to the carpings of an envious colleague who wrote in his paper that the staff of *Acontecimento* took too many taxis. The ride was brief through the narrow streets of the old city. Senhor Diocleciano lived in a house with a crumbling entrance-way. The door was opened by a plump elderly woman.

"Diocleciano is expecting you in the living-room," she said, leading the way.

Diocleciano's family living-room was a spacious apartment lit by a chandelier. The furniture, evidently bought at some discount store, was fake antique, with gilded legs and tops covered with sheets of glass. On the table in the middle of the room was a head on a dish, as in the Bible story. Firmino gave it a brief nauseated glance and turned to Senhor Diocleciano, who was seated at the head of the table as if playing host at a formal dinner.

"I fished it up at the mouth of the Douro," he told Firmino. "I had hooks out for chub and a small net for shrimp, and it got stuck on the hooks."

Firmino looked at the head on its dish, trying to overcome his repugnance. It must have been in the river some days. It was swollen and purple, one eye had been eaten by fish. He tried to give it an age, but failed. It might have been twenty, but the man could even have been forty.

"I have to turn it in at the morgue," said Senhor Diocleciano as if it were the most natural thing in the world, "so if you want to take pictures of it make it quick, because I found it at five o'clock and there's a limit to how much I can lie."

Firmino took out his camera and got busy, photographing the head full face and in profile.

"Have you noticed this?" asked Senhor Diocleciano, "come closer."

Firmino did not move. The old man was pointing a finger at one temple.

"Take a look at that."

Firmino at last brought himself to approach, and saw the hole.

"It's a hole," he said.

"A bullet hole," specified Senhor Diocleciano.

Firmino asked Senhor Diocleciano if he might make a telephone call, it would be a short one. He was taken to the telephone in the hall. At the office he got the answering service. Firmino left a message for the Editor.

"Firmino here, the severed head has been found in the river by a fisherman of corpses. I have photographed it. It has a bullet hole in the left temple. I'll send the photos at once by fax or somehow, I'll call by the Luso Agency, perhaps we can bring out a special edition, I'm not thinking of writing anything for the moment, comments are superfluous, I'll be in touch tomorrow."

He went out into the warm Oporto night. This time he had no desire whatever for a taxi, a good walk was what he needed. But not down to the river, even though it was close by. He had no wish even to look at the river that evening.

Eight

AT EIGHT O'CLOCK FIRMINO WAS awakened by the house telephone. It was the mannish voice of the moustached maid.

"Your Editor wants you on the telephone, he says it's urgent."

Firmino dashed downstairs in his dressing-gown. The pension was still sleeping.

"The presses start rolling in half an hour," said the Editor, "I'm getting out a special edition today, just a couple of pages but with all your shots, no need for a text, for the moment it's better for you to keep quiet, at three this afternoon the mystery face will be spread all over the country."

"How did the photos come out?" asked Firmino.

"Hideous," replied the Editor, "but anyone who wants to recognize them will recognize them."

Firmino felt a shiver run down his spine as he thought of the impact the paper would make: worse than a horror film. He plucked up courage and timidly enquired how the various photos would be arranged.

"On the front page we're putting the full-face shot," replied the Editor, "on the two inner pages the right and left profiles, and on the back page a postcard view of Oporto showing the Douro and the Iron Bridge, in color of course."

Firmino went up to his room. He had a shower, shaved, and put on a pair of cotton trousers and a red Lacoste T-shirt, a present from his fiancée. He gulped down a cup of coffee and went out into the street. It was Sunday, the city was practically deserted. People were still sleeping, and later on would be going to the sea. He had an urge to go there himself, even if he had no swimming trunks with him, but just to get a breath of fresh air. Then he changed his mind. He had his guidebook with him and decided to explore the city, for example the markets, the working-class parts which he didn't know. Going down the steep alleyways of the lower town he came across a bustle of activity he had not suspected. Truly Oporto kept up certain traditions which Lisbon had by now lost, such as fish-wives, even on a Sunday, carrying baskets of fish on their heads, and then the "calls" of the street trades, which took him back to his childhood: the ocarinas of the knife-grinders, the croaking bugles of the vegetable sellers. He crossed Praça da Alegria, which was as lively as its name implied. There he found a little market of green-painted stalls where all manner of things were sold: second-hand clothes, flowers, legumes, traditional wooden toys and handmade crockery. He bought a small terracotta dish on which an artless hand had painted the tower of the Clérigos. He was sure his fiancée would like it. He came to Largo do Padrao, which was a market without really being one, in that the farmers and fishermen had simply set up improvised shops in the doorways and on the pavements of Rua de Santo Ildefonso. He arrived at the Fontainhas, where he found a small flea-market. Many of the stalls were closed, because Saturday was the big day there, but a certain amount of business was done even on Sunday morning. He paused by a stall selling exotic cage-birds. On the cages were strips of paper which indicated the name of the bird and the place of origin. Most of them came from Brazil or Madeira. Firmino thought of Madeira, and how lovely it would be to spend a dream-holiday there, as promised by the advertisements for Air Portugal. Next there was a second-hand book stall, and Firmino began to browse. He came across an old book about how a city, a century ago, communicated with the world. He cast an eye at the chapter on the newspapers and advertising of the period. He discovered that at the beginning of the nineteenth century there was a paper called *O Artilheiro* in which the following fascinating announcement appeared: "Persons wishing to dispatch packages to Lisbon or Coimbra by means of our horses may deposit the merchandise at the post station opposite the Tobacco Factory." The next page was devoted to a paper called *O Periódico dos Pobres*, The Paupers' Journal, in which the ads of the tripe-vendors appeared free of charge, the sale of tripe being regarded as a public service. Firmino was overcome by a wave of affection for this city towards which, when he didn't know it at all, he had felt a certain hostility. He came to the conclusion that we are all subject to prejudice, and that unwittingly he had suffered a lapse in dialectics, that fundamental dialectic so dear to the heart of Lukács.

He glanced at his watch and thought about going to get something to eat, it was lunchtime, and he followed his nose to the Café Àncora. The place was crowded, even the restaurant part, but Firmino found a table and sat down. Almost at once the friendly waiter arrived.

"Did you find the gypsy?" he asked with a smile.

Firmino nodded.

"Later on, with your permission," said the waiter, "we'll talk about them, the gypsies, I mean. Meanwhile if you want a quick dish freshly prepared today, I recommend the octopus salad with oil, lemon and parsley."

Firmino agreed, and a minute later the waiter arrived with his order.

"Do you mind if I sit down for a moment?" he asked.

Firmino invited him to do so.

"Excuse my asking," said the waiter politely, "may I ask what job you do?"

"I'm a journalist," replied Firmino.

"Wow!" exclaimed the waiter, "in that case you can help us. Where, in Lisbon?"

"Yes, in Lisbon," confirmed Firmino.

"We're getting a movement going in favor of the gypsies of Portugal," whispered the waiter, "I don't know whether you've seen the racist demonstrations there have been in a number of towns around here?"

"I've heard about them," said Firmino.

"People don't want the gypsies," said the waiter, "in one town they've even beaten them up, it's an outbreak of racism. I don't know for sure which political parties are inciting people against them though it's not hard to imagine, and we don't want Portugal to become a racist country, it's always been a tolerant country, I am a member of an association called Citizens' Rights and we are collecting signatures, would you care to sign?"

"Willingly," replied Firmino.

From his pocket the waiter produced a sheet full of signatures headed "Citizens' Rights."

"I ought not to have you sign in the restaurant," he said, "because collecting signatures is forbidden in public places, we have special centers dotted all over town, but as the boss isn't looking, right, if you just sign here, with your particulars and the number of some official document."

Firmino wrote his name, the number of his identity card, and under the heading "profession" wrote: journalist.

"Will you give us a write-up in your paper?" asked the waiter.

"I can't promise," said Firmino, "at the moment I'm busy with another matter."

"There are some ugly things happening in Oporto," observed the waiter.

Just then a newsboy entered the café, a kid carrying a bundle of newspapers, and as he did the rounds of the tables he repeated: "The great Oporto mystery, the missing head discovered."

Firmino bought *Acontecimento*. He gave it a quick glance, folded it neatly in four because he felt embarrassed. He put it in his pocket and left. He thought he had better be getting back to Dona Rosa's.

DONA ROSA, SEATED on the sofa in the sitting-room, had a copy of *Acontecimento* open before her. She lowered the paper and looked up at Firmino.

"What a horrible business," she murmured, "the poor soul. And poor you," she added, "having to face such horrors at your age."

"That's life," sighed Firmino, taking a seat beside her.

"The pretenders to the throne are a good deal better off," observed Dona Rosa, "in *Vultos* there's a feature on a splendid reception given in Madrid, everybody is so elegant."

Just then the telephone rang and she went off to answer it. Firmino watched. Dona Rosa gave a nod, beckoning twice with her forefinger.

"Hullo," said Firmino.

"Have you something to write with?" asked a voice.

Firmino instantly recognized the voice which had called him before.

"I've got something to write with," he said.

"Don't interrupt me," said the voice.

"I'm not interrupting you," Firmino assured him.

"The head is that of Damasceno Monteiro," said the voice, "twenty-eight years old, he worked as errand-boy at the Stones of Portugal, he lived in Rua dos Canastreiros, it's up to you to find the number, it's in the Ribeira, opposite a fountain, you must inform the family, I can't do it for reasons I won't go into, goodbye."

Firmino hung up and at once dialed the number of the paper, giving a glance at the notes on his pad. He asked for the Editor but the switchboard operator put him through to Senhor Silva.

"Hullo, Huppert here," said Silva.

"This is Firmino," said Firmino.

"Enjoying the tripe?" asked Silva in sarcastic tones.

"Listen Silva," said Firmino, stressing the name, "why don't you go fuck yourself?"

There was a silence at the other end, then Silva asked indignantly: "What did you say?"

"You heard," replied Firmino, "now pass me the Editor."

After a bit of electronic music on came the Editor's voice.

"He's called Damasceno Monteiro," said Firmino, "twenty-eight years old, worked as errand-boy at the Stones of Portugal in Vila Nova de Gaia, I'll go and inform his family, they live in the Ribeira, and after that I'll go to the morgue."

"It's now four o'clock," said the Editor quite casually, "if you can manage to get me a report by nine tomorrow morning we'll come out with another special edition, today's sold out in an hour, and just think, today's Sunday and lots of the kiosks are closed."

"I'll try," said Firmino without conviction.

"You better had," declared the Editor, "and make sure

there's lots of colorful detail, plenty of drama and pathos, like a good slushy photo-romance."

"That's not my style," replied Firmino.

"Find another style," retorted the Editor, "a style *Aconteci-mento* needs. And another thing, mind it's a long piece, really good and long."

Nine

THE SCENE OF THIS SAD, MYSTERIOUS
and, may we add, bloodcurdling story is the smiling
and industrious city of Oporto. Strange but true:
Oporto, our very Portuguese Oporto, that gentle
city cradled by tender-hearted hills and traversed by
the placid waters of the Douro, on which since time
immemorial have sailed those unique *Rabelos* laden
with oaken barrels, bearing to the cellars of the city
the precious nectar which, carefully bottled and ele-
gantly labeled, will make its way to the furthest corners of the earth, enhancing the imperishable fame
of one of the most highly prized wines on the face
of the globe.

And readers of our newspaper know that this
sad, mysterious and blood-curdling story relates to
nothing less than a decapitated corpse: the pathetic
mortal remains of a person unknown, horribly mutilated, abandoned by the murderer (or murderers)
in a patch of waste land on the edge of the city, like
a worn-out shoe or an old tin pan.

This, alas, is the turn things seem to be taking
these days in this country of ours. A country which
has only recently recovered democracy and has

been accepted into the European Community along with the most civilized and progressive nations of the Old Continent. A country of honest and industrious folk, who return home of an evening weary from a hard day's work and shudder as they read of the murky deeds which the free and democratic press, such as this newspaper, is unfortunately bound to report to them, even if with aching heart.

And it is indeed with aching heart, and in great perturbation of mind, that your special correspondent in Oporto is obliged by his professional ethics to tell you the sad, murky and blood-curdling story which he himself has lived through at first hand. A story which begins in one of the many hotels in this city, where your correspondent receives an anonymous telephone call. For like all journalists engaged on difficult cases he receives dozens of anonymous calls. He answers the telephone with all the skepticism of an old and experienced journalist, fully prepared for some mythomaniac intent on telling him that a certain councilor is corrupt or that the wife of the chairman of a certain sporting club is going to bed with a bullfighter.

But not this time: the voice is crisp and almost authoritarian, with a strong northern accent: a young voice, which might well be full of self-confidence if it were not speaking in an undertone. It tells your correspondent: the head is that of Damasceno Monteiro, twenty-eight years old, he worked as errand-boy for the firm of Stones of Portugal, his home is in the Ribeira, Rua dos Canastreiros, I don't know the number because there is no number on the building, it is opposite a fountain, you must inform the family because I can't do it for reasons I won't go into, goodbye. Your correspondent is left speechless. He, an experienced, fifty year-old journalist who in the course of his life has witnessed the most appalling situations, must now take on the tragic, and at the same time Christian, task of bearing the mournful news to the victim's family. What to do? Your correspondent is fraught with misgivings, but he does not admit defeat. He knows that his profession calls even for such missions as these, painful but unavoidable. He goes down into the street, he hails a taxi and tells the driver to take him to Rua dos Canastreiros, in the Ribeira.

And here opens another scene, very different from the smiling and industrious city of Oporto, one for which the pen of the present writer is utterly inadequate, for to describe it one would need to be a sociologist, an anthropologist, which your correspondent obviously is not. This Ribeira, the slummiest part of the city, once the glorious Ribeira, seat of the artisans, the coopers, the humble folk of centuries past, lying on the banks of the Douro; this Ribeira which some superficial guidebooks for tourists attempt to pass off as the most picturesque corner of Oporto; in fact and in truth, is this Ribeira? Your correspondent has no wish to indulge in cheap rhetoric, he has no wish to fall back on illustrious literary allusions, he suspends judgment. He confines himself to describing the home, if such it may be called, of the victim's family, a dwelling like many others in the Ribeira. The hallway serves also as a kitchen, one wretched

gas ring and one faucet. A cardboard partition sepa-
rates the hallway from the cubicle which is the bedroom of Damasceno Monteiro's parents. Damasceno's own quarters are under the stairs of the
building, and can be entered only by bending low.
You find a mattress, a Mexican-type blanket, and
on the wall a poster of a Dakota Indian. The lavatory is out in the yard, and is used by everyone in
the building.

Your correspondent, the bearer of these terrible
tidings, managed to blurt out that he was a journalist from Lisbon who was engaged on the case of the
decapitated corpse. He was received by the victim's
mother, a woman some fifty years of age with the
air of an invalid. She told him that until last month
she was earning a little money by doing washing for
a few families in Oporto, but that now she had
been forced to give up working because she was suffering from internal hemorrhaging, the doctor had
diagnosed a fibroma and she had put herself in the
hands of a healer in the Ribeira who made decoctions. But the decoctions had done her no good, in
fact her hemorrhaging had increased: now she had
to go to hospital, but for the moment there was no
free bed so she had to wait. Her husband, Senhor
Domingos, was once a basket-maker, but ever since
he had stopped working he'd begun to spend every
evening in some low dive. Now he was taking
"Antabuse" because he was alcoholic. But as he was
taking "Antabuse" on doctor's orders, and at the
same time drinking cheap brandy, there were times
when he was drunk and vomited all day long. That
was him vomiting in the bedroom right now. Dam-

asceno was their only son, said the mother, Senhora Maria de Lourdes. They also had a daughter of twenty-one who had gone off to Brussels to work as a waitress in a bar, but they had had no news of her for quite a while.

Your correspondent then had to inform the poor stunned woman that her son's head was to be found in the morgue at the Institute of Forensic Medicine, and that she would be obliged to make a formal identification. The luckless mother dashed into the bedroom and returned a moment later wearing high-heeled black sandals and a fringed shawl. She said these had been a present from the singer at a nightclub in Oporto, the "Borboleta Nocturna," where her son Damasceno used to go to do small electrician's jobs, adding that these were the only decent things she had to wear.

When, after searching in vain for some means of transport, your correspondent and the poor unhappy mother arrived at the Institute of Forensic Medicine, the doctor had just removed his rubber gloves and was eating a sandwich. He was a young, friendly doctor, with a sportive air. He asked if we had come for the identification and added that he was in a hurry because that evening there was an "Invictos" roller-skate hockey-match and he was playing goalie for the "Invictos." He then took us into the adjoining room and. . .

And now I come to something I shall refrain from describing to my readers, but which they will certainly be able to imagine, and that is the reaction of the poor wretched mother. A stifled cry: Damasceno!, my Damasceno! A kind of sob, a dry rattle in the throat, a thud on the floor: the poor woman collapsed before we could come to her aid. The head, that gruesome head, was set erect on a slab of marble like an Amazonian fetish. It was cut off at the neck cleanly and precisely, as if the job had been done with an electric saw. The face was bloated and purple, because it had probably been in the river for several days, but its physiognomy was recognizable: it was that of a young man of strong and regular features in which one could still discern some measure of homespun nobility: the raven-black hair, the well-chiseled nose, the firm jaw. —Damasceno Monteiro

Dona Rosa raised her eyes from the paper, looked at Firmino and said: "You sent shivers up my spine it's so true to life and at the same time written so stylishly."

"It's not exactly my own style," Firmino tried to explain. But he was interrupted.

"But your Editor thinks the world of it," exclaimed Dona Rosa, "he says the special edition sold like hot cakes."

"Umphh," commented Firmino.

"It was brave of you," said Dona Rosa with admiration, "that's what I like, a paper with some guts, not like that rag *Vultos* that only talks about smart parties."

"My Editor tells me that our paper is going to support the Monteiro family by instituting civil proceedings in the case, and we shall need a lawyer," said Firmino. "The trouble is that we're not rolling in money, we shall need a lawyer who'll go easy on the fees, and he suggests I should ask you, Dona Rosa, because he says you will certainly know of a lawyer for our case."

"Of course I know one," Dona Rosa assured him, "when do you want to meet him?"

"Tomorrow would be fine," said Firmino.

"What time?"

"I don't know exactly," pondered Firmino, "perhaps at lunchtime, I could call on him and invite him out to lunch, but who do you have in mind?"

Dona Rosa smiled and took a deep breath.

"Fernando Diogo Maria de Jesus de Mello Sequeira," she said.

"Wow!" exclaimed Firmino, "what a name!"

"But if you call him that no one will know who you're talking about," added Dona Rosa, "you have to say Attorney Loton, that's how he's known to everyone in Oporto."

"Is that a nickname?" asked Firmino.

"It's a nickname," replied Dona Rosa, "because he looks very like that fat English actor who often played lawyer parts."

"Do you mean Charles Laughton?" asked Firmino.

"In Oporto we pronounce it Loton," said Dona Rosa. Then she added: "He comes of an old aristocratic family which in centuries past owned almost the whole region, but has now lost nearly everything. He's a genius. To judge by how he dresses you wouldn't give two cents for him, but he's a genius, he studied abroad."

"Excuse me, Dona Rosa," said Firmino, "but why should he agree to defend the interests of Damasceno Monteiro's parents?"

"Because he's the lawyer of the down-and-outs," answered Dona Rosa, "in the whole of his life he has defended no one but the really poor, it's his vocation in life."

"Well if that's how it is," said Firmino, "where can I find him?"

Dona Rosa took a sheet of paper and scribbled an address.

"Don't worry about the appointment," she said, "I'll see to that, you just go and see him at midday."

At that moment the telephone rang. Dona Rosa went to answer it, looked across at Firmino, and beckoned to him in her usual way.

"Hullo," said Firmino.

"The head has been recognized," said the voice, "so you see I was right."

"Listen," said Firmino, seizing his chance, "don't hang up, you need to talk to someone, I feel it in my bones, you have important things to say and you want to say them to me, and I would like you to do so."

"Certainly not on the phone," said the voice.

"Certainly not on the phone," said Firmino, "just tell me where and when."

There was silence at the other end.

"Tomorrow morning?" asked Firmino, "would nine o'clock tomorrow morning be all right?"

"All right," said the voice.

"Where?" asked Firmino.

"At San Lázaro," said the voice.

"What is that?" asked Firmino, "I'm not from Oporto."

"It's a public garden," came the reply.

"How will I recognize you?" asked Firmino.

"It'll be me who'll recognize you, choose a bench a bit out of the way and hold a copy of your paper on your knees, if there's anyone else with you I won't stop."

The telephone went *click*.

Ten

ON THE TRIM LAWN IN FRONT OF HIM was a grey-haired man wearing a track suit and doing gymnastics. Every now and again he set off on a timid trot, scarcely lifting his feet from the ground, and then trotted back to where a Doberman lying on the grass bade him festive welcome at each homecoming. He seemed very pleased with himself, as if he were performing the greatest feat in the world.

Firmino looked down at the newspaper prominently displayed on his knees. It was *Acontecimento*, with the headline of the special edition. Firmino folded it so as to hide the headline and leave only the name of the paper showing. He took a sweet out of his pocket, and waited. He had no wish to smoke at this hour, but for some unknown reason he lit a cigarette. In front of him passed an old lady with a shopping bag and a mother leading her child by the hand. Firmino calmly gazed at the man doing his gymnastics. And he was trying to keep his cool when a young man sat down at the other end of the bench. Firmino shot him a furtive glance. He was a youth of about twenty-five years old, wearing a workman's blue overalls and looking calmly straight ahead. The youth lit a cigarette, just as Firmino trod his out.

"He wanted to rip them off," murmured the youth, "but they ripped him off instead."

The young man said nothing more, and Firmino remained silent. A silence that seemed endless. The grey-haired man doing gymnastics passed them by with a self-assured trot.

"When did it happen?" asked Firmino.

"Six days ago," replied the youth, "at night."

"Come a bit closer," said Firmino, "I can't hear you all that well."

The young man shuffled along the bench.

"Try to tell the story logically," Firmino begged him, "and above all in the right order of events, understand that I know absolutely nothing about it, so start from scratch."

On the lawn the grey-haired man had started doing his gymnastics again. The youth said nothing and lit a second cigarette from the stub of the first. Firmino fished out another sweet.

"It was all because of the night watchman," mumbled the youngster, "because he was in league with the Green Cricket."

"Please," repeated Firmino, "try to tell the story in order."

Staring fixedly at the lawn, the youth began to speak in a low voice.

"At the Stones of Portugal, where Damasceno worked as an errand-boy, there was a night watchman, he died suddenly of a stroke, it was him who received the drugs in the containers and supplied them to the Green Cricket, and the Green Cricket sold them at the Butterfly, that is at the 'Borboleta Nocturna,' that was the circuit."

"Who is the Green Cricket?" asked Firmino.

"He's a sergeant in the Guardia Nacional," replied the youth.

"And the 'Borboleta Nocturna'?"

"'Puccini's Butterfly,' it's a discotheque down on the coast, the place is his though he's registered it in the name of his sister-in-law, the Green Cricket's a crafty one, and it's from there that the drugs are peddled to all the seaside resorts near Oporto."

"Go on," said Firmino.

"The night watchman was in cahoots with some Chinese in Hong Kong who hid the drugs in containers of high-tech equipment. The firm knew nothing about it, only the night watchman knew and of course the Green Cricket, who used to come by at night once a month to pick up the packages. But Damasceno got to know about the racket too, I don't know how. So when the night watchman had this stroke Damasceno came to my garage and said: it's not fair that the Guardia Nacional takes all that dough, tonight we'll get there first, and anyway the Green Cricket will only come by tomorrow, his day is tomorrow. I said to him: 'Damasceno you're out of your mind, you can't screw that lot, they'll get back at you, so count me out.' He turned up at my house at eleven o'clock that night. He didn't have a car so he asked me to drive him there, he was satisfied with that, for me to drive him there, and if I didn't want even to go through the gate that was all right by him, he'd do everything on his own. And he appealed to me as a friend. So I brought him there. When we arrived he asked me if I really meant to leave him to go alone. So I followed him. He walked in as if he owned the place, as if it was the most natural thing to do. He had the keys to the office, he switched on the lights and everything. He rummaged in drawers to find the code for the containers. Each container has a code to open it with. It was dead easy, Damasceno went to open the container, he obviously knew exactly where the stuff was because he was back in five minutes. He was clutching three big plastic bags of white powder, I think it was pure heroin. And also two small electronic instruments. 'Well, now that we've laid our hands on these,' he said, 'we might as well hang on to them, we'll unload them on some private clinic in

Estoril who need them?' And at that moment we heard the sound of a car."

The grey-haired man doing gymnastic exercises had met up with someone, a bob-haired woman who had greeted him as a friend, and together the two had crossed the lawn as far as the path right in front of Firmino's bench. The mature woman with the bob hairdo was saying that the last thing she'd have expected was to find him doing gymnastics in the park, and the grey-haired man replied that running a bank like his was very bad for his cervical arthrosis. The youth had stopped speaking and was looking at the ground.

"Go on," said Firmino.

"Too many people here," replied the youth.

"Let's find another bench," suggested Firmino.

"I have to make myself scarce," insisted the youth.

"Hurry up and tell me the rest then," begged Firmino.

The young man started off again in a low voice and some-things Firmino understood and some he didn't. He managed to understand that as soon as they heard a car coming the youth had slipped away into a little room. That it was a patrol of the Gardia Nacional led by the so-called Green Cricket. And that the Green Cricket had seized Damasceno by the throat and slapped his face four or five times, ordering him to go with them, and Damasceno had refused and said he'd give him away and denounce him as a drug dealer, and at that point the two other cops from the patrol had started in on him with their fists, had loaded him into the car and driven off.

"I must go," said the young man nervously, "I must go now."

"Wait a moment longer please," begged Firmino.

The young man waited.

"Are you prepared to testify?" asked Firmino cautiously.

The other thought this over.

"I'd like to," he answered, "but who'd defend a person like me?"

"A lawyer," replied Firmino, "we've got a good lawyer."

And to be more convincing he went on: "Plus the whole of the Portuguese Press, trust the Press."

The young man turned his head and looked at Firmino for the first time. He had deep, dark eyes and a meek expression.

"Where can I contact you?" asked Firmino.

"Ring the Faisca garage, electrical car repairs," said the youth, "and ask to speak to Leonel."

"Leonel who?"

"Leonel Torres," said the lad, "but I've told you those things to get it off my conscience, because I know they're the ones who killed him, but don't write that for the moment, later we might come to some agreement."

He said goodbye and left. Firmino watched him go. He was a little short, with a body too long for his too short legs. Who knows why another Torres came into Firmino's mind. But that one he'd never met, he had only seen him on a few black-and-white film clips on television. He was a positive beanpole of a Torres, who'd been his father's idol, Torres who played center forward for Benfica in the 1960s. He couldn't play football at all, his father told him, but he only had to raise his head and bang! the ball shot into the goal as if by miracle.

Eleven

IT WAS A QUARTER PAST MIDDAY. Better so, thought Firmino, who did not wish to seem anxiously over-punctual. He was walking down Rua das Flores. It was a fine street, both elegant and smacking of the common people. The note of the common people was supplied by the windowboxes blooming with geraniums, which may have been why it was called "The Street of Flowers," and the elegance by the smart jewelers' shops, their windows glittering with gems. Firmino had forgotten to bring along his guidebook, which annoyed him not a little. But never mind, he'd read up on it later.

The main door was a massive thing made of studded oak, but it had certainly seen better days. Maybe it dated from the eighteenth century. It was opened wide to allow cars in, for there was parking space at the end of the courtyard. Firmino scanned the brass plates for the name of the lawyer Mello Sequeira, but couldn't find it. He entered the atrium perplexed. There was a concierge. She sat in a glass box and was knitting. She was a concierge such as may be found in Oporto, or still perhaps even in Paris, but only in a few parts of town. She was fat, with a ballooning bosom, she had a suspicious look, she was neatly dressed after her fashion and wore slippers with pompons.

"I'm looking for Attorney Mello Sequeira," said Firmino.

"Are you the journalist?" asked the concierge.

Firmino said yes.

"The Attorney is expecting you, ground floor. There are four doors, knock at whichever you like, they're all his," said the concierge.

Firmino set off down the corridors of the old palace and knocked at the first door he came to. There was no light in the corridor, the door opened with a click, Firmino entered and closed it behind him. He found himself in a vast apartment with vaulted ceilings, though in semi-darkness. The walls were lined with books, but even the floor was cluttered with books, great tottering piles of them, along with bundles of newspapers and documents of all sorts. Firmino tried to get his eyes used to the semi-darkness. On the other side of the room, ensconced in a sofa, was a man. He was a fat man, indeed obese, of such corpulence that he filled half the sofa. At first glance he looked about sixty, perhaps a bit more. He was bald, clean-shaven, with sagging jowls and fleshy lips. His head was thrown back and he was staring at the ceiling. He really did look like Charles Laughton.

"How d'you do?" said Firmino, "I am the journalist from Lisbon."

The fat man made a vague gesture towards an armchair and Firmino sat down. On the sofa at the man's side was the latest edition of *Acontecimento*.

"Are you the author of this piece of prose?" he asked in a neutral voice.

"Yes," replied Firmino with some embarrassment, "but it's not exactly my style, I have to adapt to the style of my newspaper."

"And may I ask what is your style?" enquired the obese man in the same neutral tone.

"I try to have a style of my own," said Firmino with

mounting embarrassment, "but as you know one's style is also formed by reading the books of others."

"What others, for example, if I may make so bold?" asked the obese man.

Firmino didn't know what to say. Then he replied: "Lukács for example, Geörgy Lukács."

The fat man gave a gentle cough. He at last removed his gaze from the ceiling and looked at Firmino.

"Interesting," he said, "why? does Lukács have a style?"

"Well," said Firmino, "I think so, at least in his own way."

"And what way that be?" asked the fat man in the same neutral tone.

"Dialectical materialism," returned Firmino hastily, "let's say criticism."

The bloated figure gave another little cough, and Firmino got the feeling that those little coughs were really a kind of stifled laughter.

"Is this because, in your opinion, dialectical materialism is in itself a style?" asked the obese man, still impassive.

Firmino found himself almost at a loss. But he also felt faintly riled. This obese lawyer, unknown to him, was grilling him as if he were sitting for a university exam. Really, it was a bit much!

"What I meant," he explained, "was that Lukács's methodology is useful for the studies I am involved in, that is to say a paper I want to write."

"Have you read *History and Class Consciousness*?" enquired the obese lawyer.

"Of course," replied Firmino, "it's a fundamental text."

"It dates from 1923," commented the lawyer, "have you any notion of what was going on in Europe around that time?"

"More or less," said Firmino briefly.

"The Vienna Circle," murmured the obese man, "Carnap, the fundamentals of formal logic, the impossibility of non-contradiction within a system, trifles of that sort. As for Lukács's style, seeing that you are concerned with style, the less said the better, don't you think? Personally I think it the style of a Hungarian peasant best acquainted with horses in the Puszta."

Firmino had the urge to say that he was not there to talk about style, but he let it go.

"I need it for the study of Portuguese neo-Realism," he specified.

"Oh," yawned the obese man, "Portuguese neo-Realism, eh? Really worth studying its style, I must say."

"Not the earlier neo-Realism," Firmino went on to explain, "not the 1940s, what interests me is the second period, the 1950s, after the belated Surrealist period, I call it neo-Realism for reasons of convention, but it certainly is a different thing."

"That strikes me as more interesting," murmured the obese man, "certainly more interesting to me, but as a basis for research I would scarcely choose Lukács."

The obese man gave him a stare and proffered a wooden box. He asked if he wanted a cigar and Firmino declined. The obese man lit an enormous one. It looked like a Havana and was certainly very aromatic. He kept silent and started smoking calmly. With a lost air Firmino looked around him at that enormous room crammed with books, books everywhere, on the walls, on the chairs, on the floor, along with bundles of documents and newspapers.

"Don't you feel you are in a scene from Kafka?" said the obese man as if he had read his thoughts, "you surely must have read Kafka, or have seen the film *The Trial* with Orson Welles. Not that I'm Orson Welles, even if this den of mine is loaded with old papers, even if I am obese and smoking a fat cigar, do not muddle up your film stars, here in Oporto they call me Loton."

"So I have been told," replied Firmino.

"Let us get down to practical matters," said the lawyer, "so tell me exactly what you want from me."

"I thought that Dona Rosa had already told you everything," complained Firmino.

"Partly so," murmured the obese man.

"Well then," said Firmino, "the case is the one you have read about in my paper, even if it isn't written in a style that you like, and my paper wishes to make you a proposition: Damasceno Monteiro's family haven't got the money to pay a lawyer, so my paper has stepped in, we need a lawyer and we thought of you."

"I'm not sure," grumbled the obese man, "the fact is I'm busy over Angela, you must have heard of the case, it's in all the local press."

Firmino looked at him perplexed and confessed: "No, frankly no."

"The prostitute who was raped and tortured and practically killed," said the obese man, "the case is in the Oporto papers, I represent her. It's a pity that you of the Press follow the papers so little. Angela is a prostitute in Oporto, she was contacted for an evening of 'fun' in the provinces, she was taken by her pimp to a villa near Guimarães where a wealthy young man had her bound hand and foot by two thugs and used physical violence on her person, because this was a fancy he wanted to get off his chest but didn't know who to try it out on, so he tried it out on Angela, after all she was only a prostitute."

"Horrible," said Firmino, "and you are representing her?"

"Certainly I am," confirmed the lawyer, "and do you know why?"

"No," replied Firmino, "but I'd say to see justice done."

"Call it that if you want," murmured the obese man, "after all it's a definition of sorts. You only have to know that this sadist is the young son of a petty provincial landowner who has got rich thanks to the last few governments, the worst kind of bourgeoisie to surface in Portugal in the last twenty years: money, ignorance, and a lot of arrogance. Dreadful people who have to be reckoned with. My own family has for centuries exploited women like Angela and in some sense violated them, maybe not as this young man did, but let us say in a more elegant manner. We might even hypothesize, if you wish, that what I am doing is a kind of tardy penitence for history, a paradoxical inversion of class consciousness, not as according to the primary mechanisms of your friend Lukács, let us say on a different level, but these, however, are matters entirely my own concern, that I would prefer not to go in to with you."

"As the civil party in these proceedings," persisted Firmino staunchly, "we would like to retain you as our lawyer, if we manage to reach an agreement about your fees."

The old man emitted a couple of those little coughs that sounded like chuckles. He tapped his cigar-ash into an ashtray. He seemed amused. He made a vague sweeping gesture to indicate the room.

"This building is mine," he said, "it belonged to my family, and the next street belongs to me, belonged to my family. I have no descendants, so as long as the money lasts I can amuse myself."

"And does this case amuse you?" asked Firmino.

"That's not exactly what I wanted to say," replied the lawyer calmly, "but I would like you to be more precise about the facts in your possession."

"I have a witness," said Firmino, "I met him this morning in the public gardens."

"Is your informant prepared to give evidence before an examining magistrate?" asked the lawyer.

"I think he would if you asked him," replied Firmino.

"Come to the point," said the lawyer.

"It seems that Damasceno Monteiro was killed at the barracks of the Guardia Nacional," said Firmino point-blank.

"The Guardia Nacional, eh?" murmured the lawyer. He took a puff at his cigar and chuckled: "but in that case it's a *Grundnorm*."

Firmino gave him a bewildered look and the lawyer read his bewilderment.

"I can't expect you to know what a *Grundnorm* is," continued the lawyer, "I realize that we men of law sometimes speak in code."

"Then explain it to me," retorted Firmino, "I only studied literature."

"Have you heard of Hans Kelsen?" asked the lawyer in such a low voice that he might have been talking to himself.

"Hans Kelsen," repeated Firmino, rummaging through his scanty knowledge of jurisprudence, "I think I have heard his name, he's a philosopher of law I think, but you can tell me more about him."

The lawyer heaved such a deep sigh that it seemed to Firmino that he could hear its echo.

"Berkeley, California, 1952," he whispered. "You may not be able to imagine what California meant at that time to a young man hailing from the aristocracy of a provincial place such as Oporto and an oppressive country like Portugal, but I can tell you in a word that it meant freedom. Not the stereotyped sort of freedom you see represented in a lot of American movies of the time, even in America in those days there was fierce censorship, but genuine freedom, inward, absolute. Just imagine, I had a fiancée and we even used to play squash, an

English game then completely unknown to the rest of Europe. I lived in a wooden house overlooking the ocean, south of Berkeley, it belonged to my distant American cousins, relatives on my mother's side. But you will be wondering why I went to Berkeley. Because my family was wealthy, there's no doubt about that, but first and foremost because I wanted to study the reasons which have induced mankind to draw up codes of law. Not the codes of law such as were studied by my contemporaries who have since become famous lawyers, but the underlying, and in a sense abstract, reasons. Do you follow me? And if you don't follow me, don't worry."

The obese man paused for another puff at his cigar. Firmino became aware of a heavy fog hovering in the huge room.

"Well then," he resumed, "I set my sights on that particular man on the basis of what I had learnt as a student here in Oporto. Hans Kelsen, born in Prague in 1881, a middle-European Jew, in the 1920s he had written a treatise called *Hauptprobleme der Staatsrechtslehre*, which I had read as a student, because I am a German speaker, you know, all my governesses were German, it's practically my mother tongue. So I enrolled in his course at Berkeley. He was a gaunt man, bald and gauche, and at first sight no one would have taken him for a great philosopher of jurisprudence, they would have put him down as a civil servant. He had fled first from Vienna and then from Cologne because of the Nazis. He had taught in Switzerland and then he went to the United States. I followed him to the United States. The next year he transferred again to the University of Geneva, and I followed him to Geneva. His theories about the *Grundnorm* had become my obsession."

The lawyer fell silent, stubbed out his cigar and drew a deep breath as if he were short of oxygen.

"*Grundnorm*," he repeated, "do you grasp the concept?"

"Basic norm," said Firmino, trying to make use of the little German he knew.

"To be sure, basic principle is what it means literally," specified the obese man, "except that for Kelsen it is situated at the apex of the pyramid, it's a basic norm in reverse, it's at the pinnacle of his theory of justice, what he described as the *Stufenbau Theorie*, the theory of pyramidal construction."

The lawyer paused. He sighed again, but this time plaintively. "It is a normative proposition," he continued, "it stands on the pinnacle of what is called Law, but it's the fruit of this scholar's imagination, a pure hypothesis."

Firmino did not manage to discern whether his expression was pedagogical, meditative, or simply melancholy.

"If I may so put it," said the lawyer, "it's a metaphysical hypothesis, purely metaphysical. And if you want, this is a truly Kafkaesque thing, it's the norm that ensnares us all and which, though it may seem incongruous, might account for the arrogance of a little squire who thinks he has the right to whip a prostitute. The ways of the *Grundnorm* are infinite."

"The witness I spoke to this morning," said Firmino to charge the subject, "is certain that Damasceno was murdered by the Guardia Nacionale."

The lawyer gave a tired smile and glanced at his watch.

"Oh," said he, "now the Guardia Nacionale is a military institution, it's the very incarnation of the *Grundnorm*, this business is beginning to interest me, also because you have no idea how many people have recently been killed or tortured in our charming police stations."

"I think I have as good an idea as you do," Firmino pointed out, "the last four cases have been covered by my paper."

"Of course," murmured the lawyer, "and all the culprits acquitted, all of them comfortably back in service, this business is really beginning to interest me, but what would you say to a bite of lunch? It's half-past one and I feel a little peckish, there's a restaurant almost next door which I heartily recommend. Incidentally, do you like tripe?"

"Moderately," replied Firmino with misgiving.

Twelve

"Unfortunately, Manuel, this young man doesn't like tripe," said the lawyer to the owner when they reached the restaurant, "so please inform him of the other specialties of the house."

The owner put his fists on his hips and gave Firmino such a look that he lowered his eyes for shame.

"Don Fernando," said the owner in easy tones, "if I do not manage to meet your guest's requirements then I will offer the meal free of charge. Is he a foreigner?"

"Almost," replied the lawyer, "but he is beginning to get used to the ways of this city."

"Then I might suggest our rice with red beans and fried bass," said the owner, "or else the *roulade* of salt cod."

Firmino cast his companion a bewildered glance, wishing to indicate that either dish would suit him fine.

"Let's have both," decided the lawyer, "then we can nibble here and there. And for me the tripe, of course."

The restaurant, which was not so much a restaurant as a cellar lined with barrels, was at the end of an apparently nameless alleyway next to Rua das Flores. Over the doorway Firmino had spotted a sort of wooden inn sign crudely painted with the words: "The cellar for discerning palates is here."

"So what do you think are our next steps?" asked Firmino.

"What's the name of your witness?" asked the lawyer.

"He's called Torres," said Firmino, "he's an electrician at the Faisca Garage."

"I'll call by and pick him up this afternoon," said the lawyer, "and take him to the examining magistrate."

"And what if Torres doesn't want to testify?" objected Firmino.

"I repeat: I will take him to the examining magistrate," replied the lawyer placidly.

He poured out two glasses of a greenish wine and raised his own glass for a toast.

"This is an Alvarinho which can't be found on the market," he said, "but it's only an aperitif, after this we'll drink red wine."

"I'm not all that used to drinking wine," said Firmino apologetically.

"You can always make up for lost time," replied the lawyer.

At that moment the owner appeared with dishes of food, and addressed the lawyer as if Firmino didn't exist.

"Here we are Don Fernando," he declared with a satisfied air, "and if your guest doesn't like it the lunch is on me, as I said before, however he'd do better to quit town."

The red beans and rice, smothered in a chestnut-colored sauce, looked far from appetizing. Firmino took two fried fish and cut himself a slice of the salt cod *roulade*. The lawyer watched him with his small, questioning eyes.

"Eat up, young man," he said, "you'd better keep your strength up, this is going to be a long, complicated business."

"What should I do at this point?" asked Firmino.

"Tomorrow go to Torres" said the lawyer, "and give him a whale of an interview, as long and detailed as possible. Then publish it in your paper."

"And if Torres doesn't want to?" asked Firmino.

"Certainly he'll want to," replied the lawyer calmly, "he has no choice, the reason is simple and Torres will grasp it at once, I don't imagine he's a fool."

The lawyer took a napkin to the sauce of the tripe running down his chin, and continued in a detached tone as if explaining something absolutely elementary: "Because Torres is a finished man," he said, "this afternoon under my supervision he is going to give his evidence before a magistrate, of that I can assure you, but you know, a statement which stays in the hands of the examining authorities is a drifting mine, it's always a good rule not to trust it, that statement might come to the knowledge of someone who doesn't like it, and just imagine, with all the traffic accidents that happen these days, incidentally did you know that Portugal is at the top of the list in Europe for road accidents? It appears that we Portuguese drive like madmen."

Firmino regarded him with all the perplexity which this lawyer continued to instill in him.

"And what purpose would be served by the interview in my paper?" he enquired.

The lawyer, with great relish, devoured a strip of tripe. Although it was cut quite short he kept trying vainly to wind it up round his fork.

"My dear young man," he sighed, "you amaze me, you have been amazing me ever since you entered my house, you write for a paper with a wide circulation and you don't seem to know the meaning of public opinion, it's very remiss of you, so try to follow me for a moment. If after making his statement to the examining magistrate Torres repeats every word of it to your newspaper he can be easy in his mind, because he will have the whole of public opinion on his side, and any absent-minded driver, for example, would think twice before running over someone so much in the public eye, do you get the idea?"

"I get the idea," replied Firmino.

"And then," continued the lawyer, "and this is something that directly concerns you as a journalist, do you know what Jouhandeau said?"

Firmino shook his head. The lawyer took a sip of wine and wiped his fleshy lips.

"He said: Since the essential object of literature is the knowledge of human nature, and since there is no place in the world where one can study it better than in courts of law, would it not be desirable, by law, for there always to be a writer among the jurymen, his presence there would be an inducement to all the others to reflect more deeply. End of quotation."

The lawyer paused for a moment and took another sip of wine.

"Well then," he resumed, "it's obvious that you will never sit in the jury box of a court as Monsieur Jouhandeau wished, nor will you even be present at the preliminary enquiries, because the law does not permit it, and it is also true that strictly speaking you are not exactly a writer, but we can try to consider you as such, seeing that you write for a newspaper. Let us say that you will be a virtual juryman, and that is your role, a virtual juryman, do you grasp the concept?"

"I think so," replied Firmino.

But he wanted to come clean, so he asked: "But who is this Jouhandeau? I've never heard of him."

"Marcel Jouhandeau," came the answer, "an irritating French theologian with a taste for provoking scandal, he was also a great eulogist of abjection, if I may so put it, and of a sort of metaphysical perversion, or rather of what he imagined to be metaphysical. You must understand that he was writing in France at the time when the Surrealists were exalting rebellion and Gide had already produced his theory of gratuitous crime. But naturally he had none of Gide's stature, in fact he was pretty poor stuff, even if the occasional maxim about justice hit the mark."

"We still have to settle the basic question," said Firmino, "because my paper is naturally taking on responsibility for your fees."

The lawyer turned his inquisitorial gaze on him.

"Meaning what?" he asked.

"Meaning that your emolument will be paid in the proper manner."

"Meaning what?" repeated the lawyer, "what does that mean in numerical terms?"

Firmino felt slightly embarrassed.

"I couldn't say," he answered, "that is a question for my Editor."

"There is a house in Rua do Ferraz," said the lawyer inconsequentially, "in which I spent my childhood, it's just above Rua das Flores, a small eighteenth-century palace, the marchioness my grandmother lived there."

He heaved a nostalgic sigh.

"Where did you live as a child, in what sort of house?" he asked at length.

"On the sea at Cascais," replied Firmino, "my father was in the coast guards and had the use of a house on the sea, my brothers and I spent almost our whole childhood there."

"Ah yes," exclaimed the lawyer, "the Cascais coast, that pure white light at midday that becomes tinted with pink at sunset, the blue of the ocean, the pinewoods of the Guincho. . . . My memories, on the other hand, are of a gloomy town house, with an unfeeling grandmother who sipped cups of tea and appeared every day with a different ribbon around her wrinkled neck, sometimes simple, other times with a narrow lace trimming. She never touched me, though occasionally she lightly brushed her cold hand against mine and told me that the only thing a child had to learn about his family was to respect his forebears. I would take a look at those whom she called my forebears. They were old oil paintings of haughty men with disdainful expressions and fleshy lips like mine, which I inherited from them."

He took a mouthful of the salt cod and said: "I find this quite excellent, tell me, what do you think of it?"

"I like it," replied Firmino, "but you were telling me about your childhood."

"Very well," continued the lawyer, "that house is now abandoned, with all its memories of the old marchioness who was a grandmother to me in her way: her portraits, her furniture, her blankets from Castelo Branco and her precious family trees. Let us say that it's my childhood that is locked up there as in a casket. Until a few years ago I still used to go there to consult the family archives, but I don't know if you've seen Rua do Ferraz, to get up the slope you'd need a cable car, and with a bulk like mine I'm not up to it, I'd have to call a cab to take me five hundred meters, so it's seven years since I set foot in the place. Therefore I've decided to sell it, I've put it in the hands of an agency, it's just as well that these agencies should swallow up childhoods, it's the most antiseptic way of getting rid of them, and you cannot imagine how many middle-class upstarts, who've minted money over these last few years thanks to grants from the European Community, would like to lay their hands on that house. You see, it's a place that to their way of thinking would give them the social status which they crave, a modern villa with swimming pool in the residential areas is within their reach, but an eighteenth-century mansion in old Oporto is many steps higher up the ladder, do you grasp the concept?"

"I grasp the concept," said Firmino.

"I have therefore decided to sell it," said the lawyer. "The keenest prospective buyer comes from the provinces. He's a typical product of the society we live in nowadays. His father was a small-time cattle-breeder. He himself began with a small shoe business even while Salazar was in power. Actually he specialized in canvas footwear, with a couple of workmen. Then in 1974 came the revolution and he sided with the co-operatives, he even gave a practically revolutionary interview to a newspaper of that persuasion. Then, after the illusions of revolution, in came unbridled neo-liberalism, and he took sides with that, as he had to. In a word, he's known how to look after Number One. He owns four Mercedes and a golf course in Algarve, I believe he has shares in building projects in Alentejo, and who knows if not even in the Tróia Peninsula, he knows how to handle all the political parties in the constitutional spectrum, from the Communists to the Right, and it goes without saying that his shoe factory is flourishing, exporting chiefly to the United States. What do you say then, am I right to sell?"

"The house, you mean?"

"The house, naturally," replied the lawyer. "I might well sell it to him. A few days ago I had a visit from his wife, who I think is the only literate person in the family. I will spare you a description of that painted lady. But I raised my price, saying that I was selling the house together with its antique furniture and portraits of the old aristocracy, and I asked her: what would a family like yours do with a house like that without its antique furniture and family portraits? What do you think, young man, did I do well?"

"Very well indeed," replied Firmino, "since you ask me for my opinion I can tell you you did just the right thing."

"In that case," concluded the lawyer, "you may tell your Editor that for my expenses over Damasceno Monteiro I shall be amply remunerated by two eighteenth-century paintings in my house in Rua do Ferraz, and ask him to make no further proposals concerning my fees, if he will be so good."

Firmino made no answer but simply went on eating. He had cautiously sampled the red beans and rice and found it delicious, so he was now on his second helping. He really wanted to say something but didn't know how to put it. Eventually he tried to formulate it.

"Well my paper you know," he stammered, "or my paper is only what it is, I mean to say you know very well what its style is, it's the style we have to use to capture our readership, well it's written for the masses, it's got guts, but it's still written for the masses, it has to make concessions to its readership in short, so as to sell more copies, if you see what I mean."

The lawyer was concentrating on his food and said nothing. He was completely absorbed in eating the salt cod.

"I don't know if you grasp the concept," said Firmino, taking over the lawyer's formula.

"I do not grasp the concept," replied the lawyer.

"Well," continued Firmino, "what I mean is that my paper is the paper you know it to be, while you, well, you are a leading lawyer, you have the surname you have, and in a word I wanted to say you have a reputation to keep up, if you see what I mean."

"You continue to disappoint me, young man," replied the lawyer, "you do everything in your power to be a lesser person than you really are, we must never be less than we really are, what was it you said about me?"

"That you have a reputation to keep up," said Firmino.

"Listen to me," murmured the lawyer, "I don't think we've understood each other, so I'll tell you something once and for all, but open your ears and hear. I defend the unfortunates of this world because I am like them, and that is the pure and simple truth. Of my ancient lineage I exploit only what material inheritance is still left to me, but like the unfortunates whom I defend I think I have experienced the miseries of life, have understood them and even taken them on myself, because to understand the miseries of life you have to put your hands in the shit, if you will excuse the expression, and above all be aware of it. And kindly don't force me to be rhetorical, because this form of rhetoric is cheap."

"But what do you believe in?" asked Firmino impulsively.

He had no idea what had made him ask such an ingenuous question at that moment, and even as he spoke it seemed to him one of those questions you ask of a schoolmate, that make you both blush. The lawyer raised his head from his plate and looked at him with those inquisitorial eyes of his.

"Are you asking me a personal question?" he inquired with explicit annoyance.

"Let's call it a personal question," replied Firmino bravely.

"And why do you ask this question?" insisted the lawyer.

"Because you don't believe in anything," Firmino burst out, "I get the impression that you don't believe in anything."

The lawyer smiled. Firmino felt that he was ill at ease.

"I might, for example, believe in something that to you seems insignificant," he answered.

"Give me a convincing example," said Firmino. He had got himself into this and wanted to keep up his role.

"For example a poem," replied the lawyer, "just a few lines, it might seem a mere trifle, or it might also be a thing of the essence. For example:

> *Everything that I have known*
> *You'll write to me to remind*
> *Me of, and likewise I shall do,*
> *The whole past I'll recount to you.*

The lawyer fell silent. He had shoved away his plate and sat fumbling with his napkin.

"Hölderlin," he went on, "it's a poem called *Wenn aus der Ferne*, which means 'If From the Distance,' it's one of his last. Let us say that there might be people who are waiting for letters from the past, do you think that a plausible thing to believe in?"

"Perhaps," replied Firmino, "it might be plausible, though really I'd like to understand it a bit more."

"Nothing to it," murmured the lawyer, "letters from the past which give us an explanation of a time in our life which we have never understood, an explanation whatever it might be that enables us to grasp the meaning of the years gone by, a meaning that eluded us then, you are young, you are waiting for letters from the future, but just suppose that there are people waiting for letters from the past, and maybe I am one of these, and maybe I go so far as to imagine that one day I shall receive them."

He paused, lit one of his cigars, and asked: "And do you know how I imagine they will arrive? Come on, try and think."

"I haven't the faintest idea," said Firmino.

"Well," said the lawyer, "they will arrive in a little parcel done up with a pink bow, just like that, and, scented with violets, as in the most trashy romantic novels. And on that day I shall lower my horrible old snout to the package, undo the pink bow, open the letters, and with the clarity of noonday I shall understand a story I never understood before, a story unique and fundamental, I repeat, unique and fundamental, such a thing as can happen but once in our lives, that the gods grant only once in our lives, and to which at the time we did not pay enough attention, for the simple reason that we were conceited fools."

Another pause, longer this time. Firmino watched him in silence, taking stock of his fat old droopy cheeks, his almost repulsively fleshy lips, and the expression of one lost in memories.

"Because," the lawyer went on in a low voice, "*que faites-vous des anciennes amours?* I too ask myself this question, *que faites-vous des anciennes amours?* It's a line from a poem by Louise Colet, and goes on like this: *les chassez-vous comme des ombres vaines? Ils ont été, ces fantômes glacés, coeur contre coeur, une part de vous même.** There's no doubt the lines were addressed to Flaubert. I should add that Louise Colet wrote very bad poems, poor dear, even if she thought of herself as a great poetess and wanted to make a hit in all the literary *salons* in Paris, really mediocre stuff, no doubt about it. But these few lines really get to one, it seems to me, because what in fact do we *do* with our past loves? Push them away in a drawer along with our socks full of holes?"

He looked at Firmino as if expecting confirmation, but Firmino said not a word.

"Do you know what I say," continued the lawyer, "that if Flaubert didn't understand her then he was really a fool, in which case we have to agree with that smarty-pants Sartre, but maybe Flaubert did understand, what do you think, did Flaubert understand or not?"

"Maybe he understood," replied Firmino, "I couldn't say offhand, maybe he did understand but I'm not in a position to swear to it."

"I beg your pardon, young man," said the lawyer, "but you claim to be studying literature, indeed that you intend to write a paper on literature, and you here own up to me that you can't say anything for sure on the fundamental question,

• *"Would you send them away like useless shadows? These gelid ghosts were, heart pressed to heart, a part of yourself."*

whether Flaubert did or did not understand Louise Colet's coded message."

"But I'm studying Portuguese literature in the 1950s," Firmino defended himself, "and what has Flaubert to do with Portuguese literature in the 1950s?"

"Apparently nothing," said the lawyer, "but only apparently, because in literature everything has to do with everything else. Look, young man, it's like a spider's web, you know what a spider's web is like? Well think of all those complicated threads woven together by the spider, all of which lead to the center, looking at those at the outer edge you wouldn't think it, but everything leads to the center, I'll give you an example, how could you understand *L'éducation sentimentale*, a novel so terribly pessimistic and at the same time so reactionary, because according to the criteria of your friend Lukács it is terribly reactionary, if you don't know the tasteless novelettes of that period of appalling bad taste that was the Second Empire? And along with this, making the proper connections, what if you were to be unaware of Flaubert's state of mental depression? Because, you know, when Flaubert was shut up there in his house at Croisset, peering out at the world through a window, he was fearfully depresed, and all this, even though it seems not so to you, forms a spider's web, a system of underground connections, of astral conjunctions, of elusive correspondences. If you want to study literature at least learn that you must study correspondences."

Firmino gave him a look and tried to come up with an answer. Strangely enough he was seized with that same absurd sense of guilt the owner had caused him when he had told him what was on the menu.

"I try in all humility to concern myself with Portuguese literature in the 1950s," he replied, "without getting all swollen-headed about it."

"Right," said the lawyer, "without getting swollen-headed you have to plumb the depths of that particular period. And to do so perhaps you ought to know the weather reports published in the Portuguese papers during those years, as you may learn from a magnificent novel by one of our own authors who succeeded in describing the censorship imposed by the political police by referring to the weather reports in the papers, do you know the book I mean?"

Firmino didn't answer but moved his head in a noncommittal fashion.

"Well then," said the lawyer, "I give you that as a clue to a possible line of research, so remember, even weather reports can come in handy as long as they are taken as metaphors, as clues, without falling into the sociology of literature, do I make myself clear?"

"I think so," said Firmino.

"Sociology of literature my foot!" repeated the lawyer with an air of disgust, "we live in barbarous times."

He made to rise to his feet and Firmino leapt to his so as to get there first.

"Put it all on my bill, Manuel," called out the lawyer, "our guest enjoyed his lunch."

They wended their way out, but the lawyer stopped in the doorway.

"This evening I'll let you know something about what position Torres adopts," he said, "I'll send you a message at Dona Rosa's. But it is essential for you to interview him tomorrow and for your paper to bring out another special edition, since you are running so many special editions about this severed head, have you got me?"

"I've got you," replied Firmino, "you can count on me."

They emerged into the afternoon light of Oporto. The streets were full of bustle and steamy heat, with a light mist blurring the outlines of the city. The lawyer wiped his brow with a handkerchief and made a brief gesture of farewell.

"I've eaten too much," he grumbled, "I always eat too much. Incidentally, do you know how Hölderlin died?"

Firmino simply looked at him without answering. For the moment he really couldn't recall how Hölderlin died.

"He died mad," said the lawyer, "and that's something to bear in mind."

And supporting his enormous bulk he moved off with uncertain steps.

Thirteen

LEONEL TORRES, TWENTY-SIX YEARS OF
age, no criminal record, married with one child nine
months old, born in Braga, resident in Oporto, a
friend of Damasceno Monteiro. They were together
on the night of the murder, he has already made a
deposition to the examining magistrates. He has
agreed to grant an exclusive interview to our paper.
His statements open a new chapter in the story of
this murky case and cast disquieting doubts on the
conduct of our police. From your special correspondent in Oporto.

—*How did you come to know Damasceno Monteiro?*
I met him when my family moved to Oporto. I was twelve
years old, at that time his parents lived in the Ribeira. But not
in the same building as they do now, his father was a basket-
maker and earned good money.
—*We know that in recent months you were very close friends.*
He was in trouble and often came to my house for a meal,
he had very little money.
—*But he'd found a job not long before.*
He'd been taken on as errand-boy at the Stones of Portu-

gal, an import-export firm in Gaia, most of his work was with the containers.

—*And what had Senhor Monteiro found unusual, so to speak, about his work?*

Well, inside the containers, along with electronic instruments, there were also packets of drugs, in plastic bags embedded in stearin.

—*So you think that Damasceno Monteiro knew too much?*

I don't think it, I know it.

—*Could you explain more fully?*

Damasceno realized that the receiver was the night watchman, the old man who died a few days ago. Of course the firm knew nothing about this traffic, but the night watchman was in cahoots with these peddlers in Hong Kong, where the containers came from. He received the packets and unloaded them in Oporto.

—*What kind of drugs were involved?*

Heroin in its pure state.

—*And where did it end up?*

The Green Cricket came by and picked up the packages.

—*Excuse me, but who is the Green Cricket?*

He's a sergeant in the local commissariat of the Guardia Nacional.

—*And his name?*

Titânio Silva, known as the Green Cricket.

—*Why do they call him the Green Cricket?*

Because when he gets angry he stammers and hops up and down like a cricket. Also he has an olive-green complexion.

—*And what happened next?*

A few months ago Damasceno worked as an electrician at the 'Borboleta Nocturna,' a nightclub belonging to the Green Cricket, though he's got it registered under his sister-in-law's name. That's the base he uses to peddle all the drugs in

Oporto. The big dealers come there to buy it and then they distribute it to the mules.

—*The mules?*

The retail-pushers, the guys who sell their asses unloading the stuff around the streets, to junkies.

—*And what was it that Monteiro found out?*

Nothing special, he'd simply realized that the Green Cricket was receiving consignments of heroin from Hong Kong through an import-export firm. Could be that he'd got on their track, who knows, for the fact is that soon afterwards he got a job as errand-boy at Stones of Portugal, in whose containers the stuff arrived from Asia, and he came to realize that the receiver was the night watchman.

—*Who, it appears, has died of a stroke.*

Yes, the old man had a sudden apoplectic fit and kicked the bucket. It was such a unique opportunity: the firm's boss was abroad, the secretary on holiday and the accountant a cretin.

—*So what happened?*

So in the evening, soon after the night watchman had his stroke, Damasceno came to my house and told me that the astrall conjunction had arrived, in fact, that it would be the coup of our lives, after which we could go off to Rio de Janeiro.

—*How was that?*

Because the containers loaded with stuff had just arrived from Hong Kong, as Damasceno Monteiro well knew, and since the Green Cricket and his gang would only be coming to pick them up the next day, as arranged with the night watchman, we would rip them off and take all the stuff.

—*And how did you react to that?*

I told him he must be mad, that if we screwed the Green Cricket like that he'd have us bumped off. And apart from that, where the hell would we have sold all that stuff?

—*And what did Monteiro have to say to that?*

He said that he'd see to the sales side, he knew a good base in Algarve where they could dispatch it to France and Spain, and that it was just millions for the taking.

—*Go on.*

Well, I told him I wouldn't go with him that night, that I had a wife and baby and could get by on my pay at the garage, he told me that he was in the shit, that his father took Antabuse and was sick as a dog all night long, and that he, Damasceno, couldn't stand that life any longer and wanted to go and live in Copacabana, and since I had a car and he didn't I had to drive him there.

—*And so you drove him?*

Yes I drove him there, and to tell the truth I even went into the front yard with him, I did this of my own free will without him forcing me in any way, because I didn't like the idea of hanging around outside the gates while he went off on that dangerous errand all alone.

—*Excuse me, but put like that it sounds like a grand act of generosity on your part. Couldn't it be that at the time you were thinking more of all the money you might get out of this robbery?*

Maybe yes, I'll be frank about it. I work all day long as an electrician and earn a pittance, my home is in a basement which my wife has tried to doll up with flower-patterned curtains, but in winter the walls ooze with damp, it's an unhealthy place. And I've got a baby only a few months old.

—*So how did your friend Monteiro make out?*

He switched on the office lights as if he owned the place and told me to stay where I was, that he'd see to the rest of it. So I didn't move and took no part in the robbery. He went through the drawers until he found the codes to open the containers and then went out into the yard. I sat at the desk, I was waiting for him and didn't know what to do, so I thought I would make a free telephone call to Glasgow.

—*Excuse me, but are you telling me you actually called Glasgow from the offices of the Stones of Portugal?*

Yes, I've got a sister who emigrated to Glasgow and I hadn't heard from her for five months. You know, to call Glasgow costs quite a bit, and my sister has a little mongoloid girl, which gives her a lot of problems.

—*Please go on.*

While I was on the phone I heard the noise of a car, so I hung up and nipped into the little storeroom with a folding door where the vacuum cleaner is kept. At that moment Damasceno came in from the back yard and the Green Cricket and his gang entered by the front door.

—*What do you mean by "his gang?"*

Two members of the Guardia Nacional who never leave his side.

—*Did you recognize them?*

One of them yes, his name is Costa, he's got an enormous swollen belly because he has cirrhosis. The other I don't know, a young kid, maybe a recent recruit.

—*And what happened.*

Damasceno was carrying four packets of drugs wrapped in plastic. He realized that I'd done a disappearing act and faced up to the Green Cricket.

—*And what did the sergeant do?*

He began to hop on one leg and then the other as he does when he's mad, then he began to stutter, because as I told you when he's angry he stutters, and you can't understand a word that comes out of his mouth.

—*Then what?*

He stuttered away and said: "you son-of-a-bitch that stuff is mine." I could see him through the crack in the screen door.

Then the Green Cricket grabbed the packets of stuff and did an incredible thing.

—*What was that?*

He opened one of them with a clasp-knife, he literally ripped it open, and shook the whole contents out on Damasceno's head. He said: son-of-a-bitch, I baptize you. Do you realize what that means? He was throwing away millions and millions.

—*What next?*

Damasceno was covered with powder, as if he'd been snowed on, and the Cricket was really nervous, hopping from side to side like a devil, in my opinion he'd had a fix.

—*How d'you mean?*

That he'd had a fix. The Cricket sells the stuff, but every so often he takes it too, and he has bad stuff, like some people have bad wine, and he wanted to bump off Damasceno there and then.

—*Please make yourself clearer: bump off Damasceno in what sense?*

The Cricket had pulled out his pistol, he was hysterical, he pointed it at Damasceno's temple and then at his belly and yelled: son-of-a-bitch, I'm going to kill you.

—*Did he fire?*

He fired all right but the shot went high, it hit the ceiling, if you go to the offices of the Stones of Portugal I bet you'll be sure to find a hole in the ceiling, he didn't kill him because his men intervened and deflected the shot, and he put the pistol back in its holster.

—*What next?*

The Cricket realized he couldn't kill him there on the spot, but that doesn't mean he'd cooled off. He gave Damasceno a kick in the balls that doubled him up, then kneed him in the face, just like in the movies, and he started kicking him again and again. Then he ordered his gang to carry Damasceno to the car, they'd reckon up with him when they got him to the station.

—*What about the packets of drugs?*

They tucked them into their jackets, loaded Damasceno into the car and set off for Oporto. They were all mad with rage, like wild beasts that had smelt blood.

—*Do you want to tell us anything else?*

The rest is up to you. Next morning Damasceno's body was found by a gypsy on a piece of waste ground, he had been beheaded as you know. And now it's my turn to ask you a question: what conclusions can you draw from all this?

AND THIS IS THE question your correspondent wishes to put to all his readers.

Fourteen

DONA ROSA'S PENSION WAS quiet at that time of day. The few guests had not yet returned. In the lounge the television, at very low volume, was broadcasting a gossip program until it was time for the news.

"Let's see if the news mentions it," growled the lawyer.

The sheer bulk of the man overflowed from one of the padded armchairs in Dona Rosa's sitting-room, he drank water and mopped his brow with a handkerchief. He had only just arrived and had sat down in silence in the lounge, while Dona Rosa rushed off unbidden to fetch him a bottle of fizzy mineral water.

"I've just come from the Public Prosecutor's offices," he added, "the first interrogations have already taken place."

Firmino said nothing. Dona Rosa, moving on tiptoe, gently adjusted the antimacassars on the armchairs.

"Do you think the news will mention it?" repeated the lawyer.

"I think so," replied Firmino, "but we'll see how."

It was in fact the first item, an informative coverage which really took everything from the press, especially the interview given by Torres to *Acontecimento*, and stating that this was all they could disclose for now because of the secrecy imposed during preliminary investigations. In the studio was the inevitable sociologist who provided an analysis of violence in Europe, spoke of an American film in which a man was decapitated, and arrived at conclusions verging on psychoanalysis.

"But what's all this got to do with it?" asked Firmino.

"Just chit-chat," commented the lawyer laconically, "oh yes they're falling back on the secrecy thing, what do you say to inviting me to dinner? I feel a real need to relax."

He turned to Dona Rosa.

"Dona Rosa, what is the house offering this evening?"

Dona Rosa showed him the menu. The lawyer made no comment but appeared satisfied, for he got up and beckoned to Firmino to follow him. The dining-room was still in darkness, but the lawyer switched on the lights as if he owned the place and chose the table he wanted.

"If you have half a bottle of wine left over from lunch," he said to Firmino, "tell Dona Rosa to chuck it away, I can't stand those half-finished bottles they put on the table in some pensions. I find them depressing."

That evening Dona Rosa's cook had made meatballs smothered in tomato sauce, and the first course was green-cabbage soup. The little moustached maid entered with the steaming tureen and the lawyer told her to leave it on the table, just in case.

"You were speaking of the preliminary secrecy," said Firmino, feeling he had at least to say something.

"Ah yes," replied the lawyer, "preliminary secrecy, I'd like to talk to you about this so-called secrecy, but it would inevitably lead on to very weighty matters which might bore you, and I have no wish to bore you."

"You're not boring me in the least," replied Firmino.

"Don't you think this soup is a little too thin?" asked the lawyer, "personally I like it thicker, potatoes and onions are the secret of a good green-cabbage soup."

"Anyway you're not boring me at all," replied Firmino, "if you want to talk about such things go ahead, I'm all ears."

"I've lost my thread," said the lawyer.

"You were telling me that the matter of preliminary secrecy would have inevitably led to a more boring discussion," Firmino reminded him.

"Ah yes, of course," mumbled the lawyer.

The maid came in with the dish of meatballs and started to serve them. The lawyer had his positively smothered with tomato sauce.

"Ethics," said the lawyer while stirring a meatball around in the sauce.

"Ethics meaning?" enquired Firmino.

"Professional ethical-preliminary secrecy," replied the lawyer, "that is an inseparable binomial, at least apparently."

The meatball he was attempting to dissect flew off at a tangent and landed on his shirtfront. The maid saw all and darted over, but with a peremptory gesture the lawyer waved her away.

"Meatball and shirtfront, that also is a binomial, at least as far as I am concerned. I don't know whether or not you have realized that the world is binary, nature runs on binary structures, or at least our western culture does, which after all is the one which has catalogued everything, just think of the eighteenth century, the naturalists, Linnaeus for example, but who are we to blame him, for the fact is that this pathetic little ball rolling around in space, and on which we are traveling, is subject to an absolutely simple system, which is the binary system, what do you think about that?"

"It is," replied Firmino, "either male or female, just to be simplistic, is that the system you call binary?"

"That is the general sense," confirmed the lawyer, "from which stems truth or falsehood, for example, but that would require a really boring conversation, and as I have said I have no wish to weary you, truth or falsehood, forgive me these Pindaric flights, but this is a question of ethics, and obviously the problem of law, but I have no wish to talk about sophisticated treatises on the matter, it's not worth while."

He snorted as if in vexation, but appeared to be vexed chiefly with himself.

"Do you believe that the whole universe is also binary?" he suddenly whispered.

Firmino regarded him with astonishment.

"In what sense?" he asked.

"Binary in the way the Earth is" repeated the lawyer, "in your opinion is it binary like the Earth?"

Firmino had no notion what to answer, so he decided to hand the question back.

"What do you think?"

"I don't think so," replied the lawyer, "at least I hope not, let's say I hope not."

He caught the maid's eye and motioned to his empty glass.

"It's merely a hope," he went on, "a hope for the human race to which we belong, though a hope that in the long run doesn't concern us directly because neither you nor I will live long enough to learn what Andromeda is made of, for example, or what goes on around those parts. Just think of all those scientists in NASA and so on, working like beavers to enable our descendants in a century or two to reach places we think of as the limits of our solar system, and just imagine the faces of our poor descendants when after such a long journey they disembark from their spaceship up there and find a great big binary structure: male or female, truth or falsehood, even vice or virtue, ah yes! because the binary system, even if they weren't expecting it, calls for a priest, whether Catholic or of any other religion, to tell them: that is sinful, this is virtuous. Yes, can you just imagine their faces?"

Firmino felt the urge to laugh, but managed to confine himself to a smile.

"I don't think science fiction has ever come up with that hypothesis," he said, "I read a lot of science fiction but I don't think I've come across that one."

"Ah," said the lawyer, "I'd never have suspected you liked science fiction."

"I like it a lot," said Firmino, "it's my favorite reading."

The lawyer produced another of those little coughs of his that sounded like a chortle.

"Very well," he muttered, "and what has your friend Lukács got to do with this favorite reading?"

Firmino felt himself starting to blush. He realized that he had fallen into a trap and reacted with some pride.

"Lukács is useful to me for the study of post-war Portuguese literature," said he, "science fiction belongs to the realm of fantasy."

"That's what I wanted," rejoined the lawyer, "fantasy. It's a fine word, and also a concept to meditate upon, so meditate on it if you can spare the time. As far as I'm concerned I was fantasizing about the dessert Dona Rosa has prepared for us this evening, it's a *flan brûlé*, but maybe we'd better give up on it, just another drop of wine and I'll be off to bed because my day is over, though perhaps yours might keep going and achieve something really useful."

"Anything I can," said Firmino. "For example?"

"For example a look in at 'Puccini's Butterfly,' that's a place that might give us some interesting information. That's all. Just a little look around."

He drained his glass and lit one of his gigantic cigars.

"Use your own discretion," he went on while a match was scorching his fingertips, "take note of the people there, the employees, see whether the Green Cricket is around the place, since they've told me he keeps an office there, a chat with him might be interesting, it's really a job for the police, but can you see the police going into 'Puccini's Butterfly'?"

"No indeed," agreed Firmino.

"Right you are then," said the lawyer, "I don't want you to think of yourself as Philip Marlowe, but concerning this Green Cricket we might be able to discover something on the side, a few minor offenses, because you know what De Quincey said, don't you?"

"What did he say?" enquired Firmino.

"What he said in effect was that once a man has allowed himself to commit murder, it won't be long before he thinks it a small matter to steal, and then he'll proceed to getting drunk and to not observing the Sabbath, then to behaving like a boor and breaking his word. Once he's on that slippery slope there's no knowing where he'll end, and there are many who have to blame their ruin on some murder or other to which they had paid little heed at the time. That's what he said."

The lawyer chuckled to himself and added: "My dear young man, as I said before I have no wish to bore you, but let us suppose that I, who have just spoken to you about professional ethics, should ask for your help in piercing the so-called veil of ignorance. I'm not going to go on about it, it's the phrase of an American jurist, and it's a purely theoretical matter existing in a sort of Plato's Cave. But supposing that with my Pindaric flights I might be able to bring this concept down to the purely practical, let us say the factual level, something that no juridical theorist would ever forgive me for, and let us say that I wouldn't give a damn, what would you think?"

"That the end justifies the means," replied Firmino promptly.

"Not exactly my own conclusion," replied the lawyer, "and please don't utter that cliché again, I detest it, in its name mankind has committed the most appalling atrocities, let us merely say that I am shamelessly exploiting you, which is to say your newspaper, is that clear?"

"As clear as daylight," replied Firmino.

"And let us say that I could always justify myself with definitions provided by the theory of law, that not without some measure of cynicism I could claim to belong to the school of those who believe in the so-called intuitionist concept, but no, let us go so far as to call it an act of arbitrary fantasy, how do you like the definition?"

"I like it," said Firmino.

"In that case," said the lawyer, "with our act of arbitrary fantasy we shall work De Quincey's paradox backwards, which is to say: since I am absolutely convinced that it will not be easy to prove that the Green Cricket cuts people's heads off with electric carving knives, we shall attempt to show that he behaves anti-socially, for example that he smashes plates over his wife's head, do I make myself clear?"

"Perfectly," replied Firmino.

The lawyer seemed content. He leant back in his chair. A dreamy look came into his eyes.

"And at this point we might even introduce your friend Lukács," said he.

"Lukács?" queried Firmino.

"The principle of reality," replied the lawyer, "the principle of reality, I wouldn't be surprised if in spite of everything it might not prove useful to you this evening. But now I think you'd better be off, young man, in fact it seems to me just the right time of night for a place such as 'Puccini's Butterfly,' after which you will report everything to me in minute detail, but keep your mind concentrated on that principle of reality, I think it might be useful to you."

Fifteen

AVENIDA DE MONTEVIDEU, together with the Avenida do Brasil, combined to form an interminable seafront, far longer than Firmino had bargained for, but he had no choice but to trudge along it until he came to the nightclub, because he didn't know the number. A fresh breeze off the Atlantic ruffled the flags outside a big hotel. At first the seafront was swarming with people, mostly young families outside ice-cream parlors, with children nodding off to sleep as they sucked wearily at their ices. It occurred to Firmino that his compatriots put their children to bed far too late and maybe had too many children anyway. But then it occurred to him that that was a cretinous thing to think. He noticed that the first, crowded stretch of seafront gradually gave way to a less frequented, more classy area of austere villas and early twentieth-century buildings with iron-balustraded balconies and stuccoed façades. The ocean was pretty rough and its violent waves crashed against the cliffs.

'Puccini's Butterfly' occupied the whole of a detached building which Firmino off the cuff dated to be from the 1920s, a fine construction in the Art Nouveau style, with green-tiled cornices and verandas with small tympana in imitation of the Manueline Style of architecture. On the first-floor balcony a violet neon sign with rococo flourishes, read:

'Puccini's Butterfly.' And over each of the three entrances of
the club were other and less glaring signs indicating respec-
tively the Butterfly Restaurant, the Butterfly Nightclub and
the Butterfly Discotheque. The discotheque was the only entrance which didn't have a red carpet. The others did and were
attended quite smartly by a uniformed doorman. Firmino decided that the discotheque was not the one to aim for. It
would certainly be a place impossible to talk in, with psyche-
delic lights and deafening music. There seemed no point in
the restaurant, those meatballs would see him through the
evening. There was nothing for it but the nightclub. The doorman let him in and gave an imperceptible bow. The light inside had a bluish hue. Further down the lobby was a small bar
in old-fashioned English style, with a solid wooden counter
and red leather chairs. It was completely empty. Firmino went
through it, drew aside a velvet curtain and entered the nightclub proper. Here also the light had a bluish hue. Like a stage
servant awaiting his cue in the wings, a solicitous figure murmured in a faintly off-putting tone of voice:

"Good evening sir, have you booked?"

It was the maître d': about fifty years old, impeccable
dinner-jacket, grey hair that looked blue in that blue light, an
imposing stereotyped smile.

"No," replied Firmino, "I absolutely forgot to."

"No matter," murmured the other, "I have a good table for
you if you would care to step this way."

Firmino did so. He reckoned there were thirty tables in
the room, almost all of them occupied. Mostly by middle-
aged clients, regulars it seemed to him, the ladies rather dressy
and their squires on the whole more informal, in light linen
jackets and even a few sports shirts. There was a small stage
with a proscenium arch at the far end of the room. It was

deserted. This was plainly an interval, and through the blue-tinted room filtered some piped music Firmino thought he recognized. He cupped a questioning hand to his ear and the maître d' murmured to him, "Puccini, sir. Is this table to your liking?"

The table was in fact not too near the stage and slightly to one side, which gave him a good view of the whole room.

"Have you already dined sir, or shall I bring you the menu?" asked the maître d'.

"Can one dine here as well?" asked Firmino, "I thought the restaurant was next door."

"Here we serve only snacks," was the answer, "side dishes."

"Such as?"

"Smoked swordfish," specified the maître d', "cold lobster, that sort of thing. But would you care to see the menu or do you simply wish for something to drink?"

"Well," said Firmino vaguely, "what do you suggest?"

"You cannot go wrong with a nice glass of champagne to start with," responded the maître d'.

It occurred to Firmino that he had to make an urgent call to the Editor to telegraph more money, he had already run through his advance expenses and was living on a loan from Dona Rosa.

"Very well," he replied nonchalantly, "bring me champagne, as long as it's the best you have."

The maître d' tiptoed away. The Puccini music ceased, the lights were dimmed and a spotlight illuminated the stage. It was bluish, needless to say. In the cone of light appeared a pretty young girl, her hair done up in a chignon, and she began to sing. She sang without accompaniment, and the words were Portuguese but the tune was some kind of blues, and only after a while did Firmino realize that it was an old *fado* from Coimbra which the girl was performing as if it were a jazz number. There was some very muted applause and the lights went up again. The waiter arrived with the glass of champagne and placed it on the table. Firmino took a sip. He didn't claim to know much about champagne, but this stuff was terrible, with a sickly sweet taste. He peered around him. Everything was soft and quiet, the atmosphere was padded. The waiters moved between the tables with cat-like tread, the speakers relayed a muted *morna* by Cesária Évora, the customers chatted in undertones.

At the next table sat a man on his own, chain-smoking and staring fixedly before him at the ice-bucket with its bottle of champagne. It was genuine French champagne, Firmino noted from the label of a well-known brand. The man became aware that Firmino was staring at him and he stared back. He was about fifty with horn-rim glasses, little mustache and ginger hair. He affected a sporting air, with a mauve sports shirt and crumpled linen jacket. With shaky hand he raised his glass in Firmino's direction as if drinking his health. Firmino also raised his glass, but did not drink. The other gave him an enquiring look and brought over his chair.

"Aren't you drinking?" he asked.

"The stuff's no good," replied Firmino, "but I join with your toast in spirit."

"You know the secret?" asked the man winking, "it's to order a whole bottle, then you know what you're getting, if you just ask for one glass they give you local bubbly and charge the earth for it."

He poured himself another glass and knocked it straight back.

"I'm down in the dumps," he murmured in confidential tones, "dear friend I'm way down in the dumps."

He heaved a deep sigh and propped his head on his hand.

He looked disconsolate. He muttered: "She tells me: pull up. Just like that, without warning: pull up. And this on the road to Guimarães, which is one bend after another. I slow down and look at her and she says: I told you to pull up. She opens the door, rips off the pearl necklace I gave her in the morning, throws it in my face, gets out without a single word and slams the door shut. Have I a right to be down in the dumps?"

Firmino offered no opinion, but he made a motion that could have been a nod.

"Twenty-five years' difference in age if you get me," confided the man. "Am I right to be down in the dumps?"

Firmino was on the point of saying something but his companion went on, there was no stopping him: "That's why I came to 'Puccini's,' it's just the spot when one's feeling down in the dumps, don't you think? It's just the place to put you right again, as I don't have to tell you."

"Of course," replied Firmino," I understand perfectly, it's just the place."

The man gave a tap to the bottle of champagne and then he touched the side of his nose.

"This," he said, "we need this, that's obvious enough, but it's better through there in the 'den'." He made a vague gesture towards the far end of the room.

"Ah," murmured Firmino, "the den, yes that's certainly what we need."

The man gave another tap to the side of his nose.

"It's the best, the price is reasonable and discretion is guaranteed, but you come after me."

"The fact is," said Firmino, "I'm a bit low myself this evening, but of course I'll wait my turn."

The depressed fifty-year-old made a gesture towards a velvet curtain alongside the stage.

"*La Bohème* is just the job," he chuckled, "just the right

kind of music to raise your spirits." And once again he tapped the side of his nose with his forefinger.

Firmino got casually to his feet and edged his way round the room, keeping close to the wall. Beside the curtain indicated by the depressed fifty-year-old was another with a notice reading "Washrooms," on which were depicted two young peasants, male and female, in traditional local costume. Firmino slipped into the Gents, washed his hands and studied himself in the mirror. He remembered the lawyer's advice not to think of himself as Philip Marlowe. Really not his role, but what the depressed fifty-year-old had said was intriguing him. He left the Gents and, still with a nonchalant air, slipped behind the curtain next door. He found himself in a passageway completely muffled with carpeting, both floor and walls. He pushed ahead confidently. To his right was a padded door bearing a silver plaque engraved with the words "*La Bohème*". He opened it with a jerk and stuck his head in. It was a small boudoir with blue carpeting and wallpaper, suffused lighting and a divan. On the divan lay a man and the music was Puccini's, he thought, though he didn't know offhand which opera it came from. Firmino approached the body stretched out belly upwards and gave him a gentle cuff on the shoulder. Nothing stirred. Firmino shook him by the arm. The man didn't move. Firmino quickly left the room and closed the door behind him.

Back at his table the depressed fifty-year-old was still staring fixedly at his champagne bottle.

"You'll have to wait a while yet," Firmino whispered in his ear, "because the den is occupied."

"You think so?" asked the other anxiously.

"I'm dead sure of it," said Firmino, "there's a fellow there who's in the world of dreams."

The depressed fifty-year-old's face sagged in desperation.

"But for me it wouldn't take a minute, a couple of minutes at the most, maybe I ought to drop in on the manager right there in his office."

"Ah, certainly," said Firmino.

The man beckoned the maître d', there was a brief confabulation, and off they went together round the side of the room and disappeared behind the velvet curtain. The lights were dimmed, the girl who had previously sung the blues reappeared on the platform, entertained the public with a couple of jokes and promised to sing a *fado* of the 1930s if they would just hang on for ten minutes because, she said, the viola-player had had a slight mishap. Firmino kept his eyes riveted on the curtain. The depressed fifty-year-old emerged and passed with sprightly step between the tables. As soon as he sat down he looked at Firmino. He was no longer depressed, his eyes were shining with the light of tremendous vitality. He gave the thumbs-up sign, like a pilot signaling "chocks away."

"Feeling fit?" enquired Firmino.

"Twenty-five years younger than me, but she was a little whore," mumbled the man, "except that it took a moment's thought for me to realize it."

"A rather expensive moment," murmured Firmino.

"Two hundred dollars well spent," said the bloke, "really cheap at the price, especially considering the secrecy."

"As a matter of fact it's not all that expensive," said Firmino, "but worse luck I left my roll of dollars at home."

"Senhor Titânio accepts nothing but dollars, friend," said the fifty-year-old, "just think of his position and all the risks he has to run, would you accept Portuguese escudos if you were in his shoes?"

"Not on your life," Firmino assured him.

"Well if you booked for *La Bohème*," said the man, "it's tough luck on you."

Firmino looked at his bill and counted out the exact amount. Luckily, payment was in escudos. He had an urge to walk the whole length of the seafront, he was sure that a breath of fresh air would do him a world of good.

Sixteen

FIRMINO ENTERED THE COURTYARD of the house in Rua das Flores and passed the concierge's cubbyhole. The woman gave him a quick glance and plunged back into her knitting. Firmino crossed the corridor and rang the bell. As before, the door clicked open.

Don Fernando was seated at a green baize table, practically perched on a chair too small to contain his bulk, with a game of patience set out before him. His cigar was alight, but burning itself slowly out in an ashtray. The room smelt of mold and stale tobacco-smoke.

"I'm playing Spite and Malice," said Don Fernando, "but it's not coming out, I'm not on form. Do you know how to play Spite and Malice?"

Firmino stood stock-still before him with a sheaf of newspapers under his arm, watching the old lawyer in silence.

"They call them games of patience," said Don Firmino, "but the definition is inexact, they require instinct and logic, as well as luck of course. This is a variant of Milligan, though perhaps you don't know Milligan either."

"Frankly no," replied Firmino.

"Milligan," explained Don Fernando, "is played with several players and two packs of fifty-two cards and stacks in sequence, the opening is made with the ace or the queen, with the ace the stack goes in ascending order, and in descending order if the queen opens, but that is not the best part, the beauty of it is in the obstacles."

The lawyer picked up the cigar, which already had an inch of ash on it, and took a voluptuous puff. "You really ought to study these so-called games of patience," he resumed, "some of them have mechanisms resembling the intolerable logic that conditions our life, and Milligan is one of them. But do sit down, young man, please take that chair."

Firmino sat down and placed his sheaf of newspapers on the floor.

"This Milligan is very interesting," said the lawyer, "based as it is on the moves each player makes to set traps and restrict the choices of the next player, and so on round the table, as at international conferences at Geneva."

Firmino stared at him, his face taking on an expression of bewilderment. He made a rapid, fruitless attempt to decipher the lawyer's meaning.

"Conferences at Geneva?" he queried.

"The fact is that a few years ago," said the lawyer, "I asked to be an observer at the discussions on nuclear disarmament which regularly took place at the United Nations Headquarters in Geneva. I struck up a friendship with a certain lady, the ambassadress of a country in favor of disarmament. So I came to learn that her country, at that time carrying out nuclear experiments, was also committed to worldwide abolition of atomic weapons, do you grasp the concept?"

"I grasp it," said Firmino, "it's a paradox."

"Well then," continued the lawyer, "this was a lady of considerable culture and knowledge, as you may suppose, but above all she was a passionate card-player. One day I asked her to explain to me the mechanism of those negotiations, since this eluded my sense of logic. Do you know what she answered?"

"I can't imagine," replied Firmino.

"That I should study Milligan," said Don Fernando, "because the logic was the same, and that is that every player who pretends to be collaborating with another is in fact constructing a sequence of cards which will trap his opponent and limit his choices. What do you think of that?"

"Some game," replied Firmino.

"You've said it," agreed Don Fernando, "but that's what the nuclear balance of our planet rests on—on Milligan.

He tapped the top of one of the stacks of cards.

"But I play it on my own, introducing the variant of Spite and Malice, it seems to me more appropriate."

"Meaning what?" asked Firmino.

"That I play a game of patience in such a way as to be at the same time myself and my opponent, I think the situation requires it, being concerned with missiles to be launched and others to be avoided."

"One missile we have got," declared Firmino, evidently pleased with himself, "it hasn't got a nuclear warhead but it's better than nothing."

Don Fernando broke up his game of patience and collected the cards one by one. "You interest me, young man," he said.

"At 'Puccini's Butterfly,'" said Firmino, "drugs are not only peddled but consumed on the premises. In the corridor at the back there are private rooms, complete with comfortable sofas and operatic music, I think it is mostly cocaine but there could be other stuff as well, a sniff costs two hundred dollars, and the man who runs the show is certainly Titânio Silva. Shall I shoot him down in our paper?"

The lawyer got to his feet and crossed the room unsteadily. He stopped near an Empire-style console on which stood a framed photograph which Firmino had not noticed before. He propped an elbow on the marble top of the console, assuming an attitude which to Firmino appeared theatrical and almost as if he were addressing a court of law.

"You are a good reporter, young man," he exclaimed, "within certain limits of course, but don't go doing a Don Quixote on me, because Sergeant Titânio Silva is a very dangerous windmill. And since we well know that our gallant Don Quixote got the worst of it when he was caught up in the sails of the windmill, and since I cannot and have no wish to be his Sancho Panza anointing his poor bruised body with balsamic oils, I will tell you one thing only, so listen carefully. Listen carefully because it's of basic importance as a move in our game of Milligan. You will now proceed to draw up an exhaustive statement to send to a press agency, describing 'Puccini's Butterfly' in the minutest detail, with its little cozy dens, its operatic music, its packets of various substances and dollars accurately added up by the efficient cashier Titânio Silva, all this, I say, will be reported *en bloc* by the Portuguese press, all the papers possible or imaginable, that part of it which espouses the magnificent and progressive destinies of the human race and also the sector devoted to the sports cars owned by the petty manufacturers of the North, which after all just means another way of conceiving the magnificent and progressive destinies, in short, every paper in its own way will be forced to publish this story, some with savage rage, others scandalized, others again with reservations, but they will all have to write that probably, and I repeat probably, in the face of incontestable evidence, on those premises, with perfect impunity, on account of the curious forgetfulness of the Republican Guardia Nacional, which has never taken it into its head to search them, are peddled certain oneirizing powders, how's that for a description? at the modest price of two hundred dollars a sniff, which is to say a third of the monthly wage of the average Portuguese worker. In this way we will bestow on

'Puccini's Butterfly,' and obviously also on Senhor Titânio, the privilege of a search by the criminal investigation department."

The lawyer paused as if to draw breath. And draw it he did, like a drowning man, and the sound he made was like a pair of old bellows.

"It's all the fault of these *puros*," said he, "I have to smoke these Spanish *puros* because you can't get Havanas any more, they've become a memory, but perhaps that island itself has become a mere memory." Then he continued: "We are straying from the point, though in fact it is only I who am straying from the point, please forgive me, I have too many things buzzing about in my head today."

The hand on which his chin was resting was all the while fingering his flabby cheek.

"And then I slept badly, I have too many sleepless nights, and sleepless nights bring ghosts with them and make time recoil. Do you know what it means when time recoils?"

He looked questioningly at Firmino, and Firmino once again felt nettled and embarrassed. He didn't at all like the way Don Fernando treated him, and perhaps others, as if he were looking for an accomplice, as if expecting a confirmation of his doubts, but in an almost threatening manner.

"I don't know what you mean, sir," he said, "you talk in such an ambiguous way, I don't understand what you mean by time recoiling."

"I realize," murmured the lawyer, "that you are not the right person to talk to on the subject of time. Of course, you are young, and for you time is a ribbon stretching out before you, you are like a driver on an unknown road, whose only interest is in what will happen after the next bend. But that was not what I meant to say, I was referring to a theoretical concept, hell and dammit, who knows why theories have such a hold on me, perhaps because I practice law, and that too is one enormous theory, a shaky edifice surmounted by an infinitely great dome, like the celestial vault which we may observe while comfortably seated in a planetarium. You know, I once happened to come across a treatise on the theory of physics, one of those elucubrations thought up by mathematicians cloistered in comfortable cells in universities, and it spoke of a time, and one phrase really struck me and made me think, a phrase which said that at a certain time, in the universe, time came into existence. This scientist perfidiously added that this concept cannot be grasped by our mental faculties."

He looked at Firmino with his small inquisitorial eyes. He shifted his position. He now thrust his hands into his pockets, in the attitude of a street urchin taunting someone.

"I do not wish to appear presumptuous," he said with a provocative air, "but such an abstract concept needed a translation into human terms, do you understand me?"

"I'm doing my best," responded Firmino.

"Dreams," resumed the lawyer, "the translation of theoretical physics into human terms is possible only in dreams. Because in fact the translation of this concept can occur only here, right inside here."

And he tapped his temple with a forefinger.

"Here in our little heads," he went on, "but only when they are sleeping, in that uncontrollable space which according to Dr. Freud is the free state of Unconscious. It is true that that formidable sleuth could not make a connection between dream and the theorem of theoretical physics, but it would be interesting if someone did it some day. Do you mind my smoking?"

He tottered to the little table and lit one of his cigars. He took a puff without inhaling and blew some smoke rings.

"I sometimes dream about my grandmother," he said pensively, "all too often I dream about her. She was very important to my childhood, you know, I was practically brought up by her, even though I was really in the hands of governesses. And sometimes I dream of her as a child. Because, to be sure, even my grandmother was once a child. That terrible old woman, as fat as I am now, with her hair all done up in a bun and a velvet ribbon round her neck, and her black silk dresses, her way of staring at me without a word when she made me have tea with her in her apartments, well, that fearsome woman who was my waking nightmare has now entered my dreams, and she has entered them as a child, what a strange thing to happen, because I could never have imagined that the old harridan had once been a child, but a child she is in my dream, in a little blue dress as light as a cloud, with bare feet, and curls tumbling on to her shoulders: and they are blond curls. I am on the other side of a stream and she is trying to reach me by setting her rosy little feet on stones in the running water. I know that she is my grandmother, but at the same time she is a little girl, just as I am a little boy. I don't know if I have explained myself. Have I?"

"I wouldn't know," replied Firmino cautiously.

"I haven't," continued the lawyer, "because dreams can't be explained, they don't take place within the sphere of the expressible, as Dr. Freud would have us believe, all I wanted to say was that time can begin in this way, in our dreams, but I didn't manage to say it."

He stubbed out his cigar and heaved one of those enormous sighs that sounded like a pair of bellows.

"I am tired," he said, "I need to take my mind off things, I do have more concrete matters to speak to you about, but for the moment we have to go out."

"I walked here," Firmino pointed out, "as you know I have no means of transport."

"Well I won't walk for sure," said Don Fernando, "with all this flab on me it exhausts me to walk, perhaps we can get Manuel to drive us, if he's not too busy there in his cellar, he's the one who acts as my chauffeur on rare occasions, he looks after my father's car, it's a Chevy from the 1940s but in perfect order, the engine runs as smooth as oil, we could ask him if he'll take us for a ride."

Firmino realized that the lawyer was waiting for his approval, so he nodded hastily. Don Fernando picked up the telephone and called Senhor Manuel.

"IT ISN'T EASY TO ESCAPE from Oporto," said the lawyer, "but maybe the real problem is that it isn't easy to escape from ourselves, if you will excuse the triteness."

The car was humming along the coast road, Senhor Manuel was driving very carefully, darkness had fallen and on their left the lights of the city were already distant. They passed an enormous slate-roofed building, the lawyer waved a vague hand towards it.

"That's the old headquarters of the Electricity Company," he said, "what a grim building, eh? now it's a sort of depository for all the memories of the city, but when I was a child and they took me to the farm electric light had not yet arrived in the countryside, people made do with oil-lamps."

"There at the Horse Farm?" asked Manuel over his shoulder.

"Yes, at the Horse Farm," replied the lawyer.

He wound down the window and let in a bit of air.

"The Horse Farm is my early childhood," he said in a low voice, "the first years of my life were spent there, my German governess took me into the city for Sunday tea with my grandmother, the woman who was a substitute mother to me lived at the farm, her name was Mena."

The car crossed a bridge and turned right onto a road with

little traffic. At the turning the headlights showed a couple of signposts: Areinho, Massarelos. Places Firmino had never heard of.

"When I was a child it was a flourishing farm," said the lawyer, "and they called it the Horse Farm because there were horses for the most part, but also mules and pigs. No cows, because the farm managers kept the cows on the farms up north, near Amarante. Down here it was mostly horses."

He sighed. But this time the sigh was hushed and muted, almost imperceptible.

"My wet-nurse was called Mena," he continued in a whisper. "That was a diminutive, but I always called her Mena, Mamma Mena, a Junoesque woman with breasts that could have suckled ten babies, and there I sought comfort, the bosom of Mamma Mena."

"Happy memories in fact," observed Firmino.

"Mena died too young alas," continued the lawyer, ignoring what Firmino had said, "and I have given the farm to her son, making him promise to go on keeping a few horses, and he still has three or four, even if he makes a loss on them, he only does it to comply with this whim of mine, so that I still feel myself to be in my childhood home, where I can take refuge when I feel the need for comfort and contemplation. Jorge, Mamma Mena's son, is the only relative I have left, he's my foster-brother, and I can come to his house any time I like. So you see, young man, you are very privileged this evening."

"I am well aware of it," replied Firmino.

Senhor Manuel turned down a narrow dirt road where the car left a cloud of dust in its wake. This dirt road ended at a yard on the other side of which rose a traditional old farmhouse. Under the arches an elderly man was waiting. The lawyer got out of the car and embraced him, Firmino shook his hand, the man murmured some words of welcome, and

Firmino realized that this was Don Fernando's foster-brother.
They entered a rustic room with a beamed ceiling where there
was a table laid for five. Firmino was invited to take a seat
while Senhor Jorge led the lawyer into the kitchen. When they
returned they were each carrying a glass of white wine, and the
girl who followed in their wake filled all the glasses.

"This wine comes from the farm," explained the lawyer,
"my brother sells wine for export, but you won't find this vintage on the market, it's strictly for home consumption."

They drank a toast and took their places at the table.

"Ask your wife to join us," said the lawyer to Senhor Jorge.

"You know she'd be embarrassed," replied Senhor Jorge,
"she'd rather eat in the kitchen with the girl, she says it's men's
talk."

"Bring your wife in," said Don Fernando firmly, "I want
her to sit at table with us."

The wife came in bearing a laden tray, gave a little bow and
sat down without a word.

"Spare-ribs," said Jorge to Don Fernando almost apologetically, "but you telephoned at the last moment, it's the best
we could get ready in time. The pork isn't our own, but you
can trust it."

During supper no one said very much. A bit of chat about
the weather, the sweltering heat, and how the traffic had become impossible, things of that sort. Then Senhor Manuel
dared a teasing remark: "Ah, Jorge my friend, if only I could
have a cook like yours in my restaurant. . ."

"My cook is my wife," said Senhor Jorge ingenuously. The
conversation ended there.

The girl who had poured out the wine came back and
served coffee.

"She's Joaquim's granddaughter," said Jorge turning to
Don Fernando, "she spends more time at our house than at

her own, do you remember Joaquim? He suffered a lot before he died."

The lawyer nodded but said nothing. Senhor Jorge uncorked a bottle of grappa and filled everyone's glass.

"Fernando," he said, "Manuel and I will stay here and chat, we have a lot to say to each other about vintage cars, if you want to take your guest to see the horses by all means do so."

Don Fernando got to his feet with his glass of grappa in his hand and Firmino followed him out of the house. It was a starry night and the sky was luminous beyond belief. From behind the hill rose the reflection of the lights of Oporto. The lawyer took a few steps into the yard with Firmino close beside him. He raised one arm and made a sweeping gesture round the yard.

"Quinces," he said, "all round here once upon a time there used to be quince trees. The pigs used to guzzle underneath them because there were masses of windfalls. Mena used to make quince jam in an old black pot hung over the kitchen fire."

On the other side of the yard were the dark outlines of the stables and barns. The lawyer made for them with his lumbering gait.

"Does the name of Arthur London mean anything to you?" he murmured.

Firmino gave it a moment's thought. Answering one of this lawyer's unpredictable questions he was always scared of making a blunder.

"Wasn't he a big Czechoslovakian politician tortured by the Communists there?" was all he came up with.

"To make him swear to a lie," added the lawyer, "and later he wrote a book about it, it's called *The Confession.*"

"I've seen the film," said Firmino.

134 • ANTONIO TABUCCHI

"That'll do," murmured the lawyer, "his most brutal jailers were called Kohoutek and Smola, those are their very names."

He opened the stable door and entered. There were three horses inside, one of which stamped a little as if in alarm. Above the doorway was the kind of blue light bulb you find in trains. The lawyer sat heavily down on a bale of straw. Firmino followed his example.

"I love the smell of this place," said Don Fernando, "whenever I feel depressed I come here, I breathe in this smell and look at the horses."

He slapped his enormous belly.

"I believe that for a man like me, with such a repulsively deformed body, simply to look at the beauty of horses is a kind of consolation, it gives us faith in nature. Incidentally, does the name of Henri Alleg mean anything to you?"

Firmino was once again caught unawares. He preferred to say nothing, and simply shook his head in the semi-darkness.

"A pity," said the lawyer, "he was a colleague of yours, a journalist, and in a book called *La Question* he tells us how in 1957 he was accused by the French army in Algeria of being a Communist and pro-Algerian, and he, a European and Frenchman, was tortured in Algiers to make him reveal the names of the other pro-Algerian partisans. To recapitulate, Arthur London was tortured by the Communists, Henri Alleg was tortured because he was a Communist. Which goes to show that torture can be practiced by all parties, and this is the real problem."

Firmino said nothing. One of the horses gave a sudden neigh, and to Firmino's ears it was a disquieting sound.

"Alleg's jailer was called Charbonnier," went on the lawyer almost in a whisper, "he was a lieutenant in the paras, it was he, Charbonnier, who gave electric shocks to Alleg's testicles. I have a mania for remembering the names of torturers, for some reason remembering the names of torturers means something to me, and do you know why? because torture is an individual responsibility, to say you're obeying orders from above is inexcusable, too many people have used that shabby excuse to shield themselves by legal quibbles, do you follow me? They hide behind the *Grundnorm*."

He heaved an enormous sigh, which a horse acknowledged by pawing the ground angrily.

"Many years ago, when I was young and full of enthusiasm, and still thought that writing served some purpose, it entered my head to write about torture. I came back from Geneva, and at that time Portugal was a dictatorship and under the thumb of the Political Police, a body of men who knew exactly how to extort confessions, if you understand me. I had a pretty good field of enquiry available right here in Portugal, the Portuguese Inquisition, and I started to delve into the archives of the Torre do Tombo. I can assure you that the refined methods of the jailers who tortured people in our country for centuries are of truly special interest, so learned they were about the muscles of the human body, as studied by the great anatomist Vesalius, to the reactions of the principal nerves which traverse our limbs, our poor little genitals, a perfect knowledge of anatomy, and all done in the name of the *Grundnorm*, and you can't get more *Grundnorm* than that, the Absolute Norm, you follow me."

"Meaning what?" enquired Firmino.

"Meaning God," responded the lawyer. "Those diligent, highly refined torturers were working in the name of God, from him they had received the orders from above, the concept is practically the same: I am not responsible, I am a simple sergeant, I've had orders from my captain, I am not responsible, and I am only a humble captain, I've had orders from my general, or from the Government. Or else from God. The most unbeatable thing."

"But all the same you wrote nothing?" asked Firmino.

"I gave up on it."

"Forgive me for asking," said Firmino, "but why?"

"Who knows?" answered Don Fernando, "perhaps it seemed to me fruitless to write against the *Grundnorm*, and in any case I'd read an essay on torture by a very bumptious German writer, and it made up my mind for me."

"Forgive my asking," said Firmino, "but do you read only German writers?"

"Mostly," replied Don Fernando, "because even though I grew up in Portugal it may be that culturally speaking I am really German, that was the first language I learnt to express myself in. The author of that essay was called Alexander Mitscherlich, he was a psychoanalyst, because unfortunately even psychoanalysts have started to busy themselves with these problems, and he came up with the image of Christ Crucified, and stated that it is an image closely connected with our culture, and in some way he uses this to maintain that if in the Unconscious death itself is not a sufficient punishment, then it comes down to this: don't let's kid ourselves, torture is here to stay, because we cannot suppress the destructive impulses of mankind. To put it more briefly, we'd better resign ourselves because *l'homme est méchant*. For all his Freudian theories that's all this fellow had to say: that mankind is wicked. I therefore made a different choice."

"And what was that?" asked Firmino.

"To dump theory and put things into practice," said Don Fernando, "it is humbler to go into court and defend those who undergo such treatment. I couldn't say whether it's more useful to write a treatise on agriculture or to break up a clod of earth with a mattock, but I decided to work with the mattock, like a peasant. I spoke of humility just now, but don't put too much faith in that, because when it comes down to it my attitude is more one of pride."

"Why are you telling me all this?" asked Firmino.

"Damasceno Monteiro was tortured," said the lawyer quietly, "he has the marks of cigarette burns all over his torso."

"How do you know that?"

"I asked for a second autopsy," replied Don Fernando, "at the first autopsy they failed to report this small detail."

He took a deep breath and emitted an asthmatic wheeze.

"Let's go outside," he said, "I need some fresh air. But in the meanwhile you must report this in your newspaper, naturally from an unknown source, but you must inform public opinion at once, and in two or three days' time we may speak of the so-called secrecy covering the investigations now under way, but let's go one step at a time."

They went out into the yard, Don Fernando raised his head to look at the vault of the heavens.

"Millions of stars," he said, "millions of nebulae, fuck, millions of nebulae, and here we are fretting about electrodes applied to people's genitals."

Seventeen

SEATED IN AN ARMCHAIR IN THE lounge, Dona Rosa was sipping a cup of coffee. It was ten in the morning. Firmino knew that he was still looking a bit glassy-eyed, in spite of the quarter-of-an-hour spent under a warm shower to try and wake himself up.

"My dear young man," said Dona Rosa affably, "come and have a cup of coffee with me, I never manage to catch a glimpse of you."

"Yesterday I was at the botanical gardens," apologized Firmino, "I spent the whole day there."

"And the day before?"

"At the museum, and later at the cinema, they had a film on that I'd missed in Lisbon," responded Firmino.

"And the day before that?" persisted Dona Rosa with a smile.

"With Don Fernando," said Firmino, "in the evening he took me out to dine in the country, at a farm of his."

"It is no longer his property," corrected Dona Rosa.

"So he told me," replied Firmino.

"And what did you find to interest you so much in the botanical gardens?" asked Dona Rosa. "I have never been there, I'm so housebound."

"A hundred-year-old dragon tree, it's an enormous tropical

palm, there are very few specimens in Portugal, it seems it was planted by Salabert in the nineteenth century."

"You know so much, dear boy," exclaimed Dona Rosa, "but of course in your profession you need a lot of knowledge, tell me then, who was this gentleman with the foreign name who planted this tree?"

"It's not that I know all that much," replied Firmino, "I read it in my guidebook, he was a Frenchman who came to Oporto when Napoleon invaded us, I think he was an officer in the French army, and he it was who founded the botanical gardens here in Oporto."

"The French are a cultured people," said Dona Rosa, "their republican revolution came much earlier than ours did."

"We only became a republic in 1910," rejoined Firmino, "every country has its own history."

"Yesterday on TV I saw a program on the monarchies of Northern Europe," said Dona Rosa, "they're on the ball, those people, they have an altogether different style."

"They also stood up against the Nazis," said Firmino.

Dona Rosa uttered a little cry of surprise.

"I didn't know that," she murmured, "so you can tell they're on the ball then."

Firmino finished his coffee and got up, saying that if she would excuse him he had to go and buy the papers. Dona Rosa, beaming all over her face, pointed to a stack of newspapers on the divan.

"They're all here," she said, "fresh off the press, Francisca went to buy them at eight o'clock, it's a terrific scandal, the whole press is talking about it, this Titânio is up against it in a big way, if it hadn't been for you journalists the police would never have gone near the place, so thank God for the Press, say I."

"In all modesty, we do what we can," responded Firmino.

"Don Fernando telephoned at nine o'clock," Dona Rosa informed him, "he needs to speak to you, actually he has put everything in my hands, but I think it's best for you to talk to him first."

"I'll go and see him at once," said Firmino.

"I would advise against that," said Dona Rosa, "Don Fernando can't receive you today, he's having one of his crises."

"What sort of crises?"

"Everyone can have their little crises," replied Dona Rosa gently, "so it's better not to go disturbing him, but don't worry, he said he'd call you back and give you instructions, all you need is a little patience."

"I've got patience enough," said Firmino, "but I'd have liked a short stroll, perhaps as far as the Café Centrale."

"I can see that what you need is a cup of good strong coffee," said Dona Rosa affectionately, "this stuff Francisca makes in the morning is full of barley, what you need is a good strong espresso so I'll go and get her to bring you one, meanwhile you stay here and read all the big news about that nightclub, then before long we'll take a peek at the television, there's a program on nature, I don't know if you've ever seen it but it fascinates me, it's presented by a really nice scientist at Lisbon University, and today's program is all about the chameleon of the Algarve, it seems that the Algarve is one of the few places in Europe where the chameleon has managed to survive, so it says on the TV page."

"In my opinion chameleons manage to survive everywhere," quipped Firmino, "all they have to do is change color."

"You took the words right out of my mouth," laughed Dona Rosa, "and you must know more about that kind of chameleon than I do, what with your work, I scarcely ever leave the house, but believe me even I know a few chameleons, specially in this city."

The television screen showed a lagoon with a white beach and humpy sand dunes. Firmino thought it looked like Tavira, and it may indeed have been in those parts. Then the camera swiveled to a hut on the beach, which was a restaurant with a few plastic tables outside it, at which some blond foreigners sat eating clams. The camera zoomed in on a freckly faced girl and the commentator asked her what she thought of the place. She answered in English, and Portuguese subtitles appeared on the screen. She said that beach was an absolute paradise for someone like her, coming from Norway, the fish was fantastic and a whole seafood meal cost the same as two cups of coffee in Norway, but the main reason why she was eating at that shack was Fernando Pessoa, and she pointed to a branch of the pergola which shaded the place. The lens focused on the branch, and there in close-up, dead still but with large eyes darting this way and that, was a giant lizard which looked like part of the branch. It was one of the poor surviving chameleons of the Algarve. The commentator then asked the Norwegian girl why the reptile was called Fernando Pessoa, and she told him she had never read any of that poet's works but that she knew he was a man of a thousand different masks, and that like the chameleon he camouflaged himself with every sort of disguise, and that was why the owner of the restaurant had made that his signboard. The camera then shifted to a hand-painted sign over the hut, on which were the words: "Chameleon Pessoa."

At that moment the telephone rang and Dona Rosa motioned to Firmino to answer it.

"I have a couple of things to tell you," came the lawyer's voice, "have you got pen and paper?"

"I've got my notebook right here," replied Firmino.

"They're contradicting themselves," said the lawyer, "take notes because this is important. In the first version they denied having taken Damasceno to the police station. Unfortunately for them they were given the lie by the witness, who, get this one, had followed them in his own car. They had previously said they had let Damasceno out of the car along the way, whereas Torres, who had followed them at a discreet distance all the way to Oporto, maintains that with his own eyes he saw Damasceno being beaten up on the way into the station. Now comes a second contradiction: they were forced to admit that they had taken Damasceno to the station for a mere check-up, and that they had detained him only for a short while, the time needed to check his papers and so on, half an hour at the most. Therefore, supposing they got there at about midnight, at around half-past twelve Monteiro would have walked out of there on his own two feet. You follow me?"

"I follow you," Firmino assured him.

"But the fact is that Torres, who seems a tough egg," continued the lawyer "states that he stayed there in his car until two o'clock in the morning, and never saw Damasceno Monteiro come out. You follow me?"

"I follow you," confirmed Firmino.

"Therefore," affirmed the lawyer, "Monteiro was there in the station at least until two o'clock, at which time Torres thought he had better go back and off he went. And it's at this point that things become more of a muddle, for example, the orderly responsible for registering arrival times, was at that time sleeping like a child with his head on the desk, and there's also the story of some coffee which the Green Cricket went down to the kitchen to prepare with the help of one of his men. With things of this sort they managed to string together a slightly more convincing yarn, which is the final version, the one the Green Cricket is bound to use at the trial. But it is not up to me to tell you this version."

"Who's going to tell me then?" asked Firmino.

"You will learn it directly from Titânio Silva," replied the lawyer. "I am dead sure that this is his final version, and also what he will say at the trial, but this is a statement which it would be better for you to hear from his own lips."

From the receiver came a kind of wheeze followed by a few coughs.

"I have an attack of asthma," explained the lawyer with the same wheeze in his voice, "my attacks of asthma are psychosomatic, crickets secrete a fine powder beneath their wings and this brings on an attack."

"What must I do?" asked Firmino.

"I promised to have a talk with you about professional ethics," replied the lawyer, "so you may consider this telephone call as the first practical lesson. Meanwhile, in your newspaper, stress the contradictions into which these men have fallen, it is a good thing for public opinion to get the idea, and as regards this latest version go and interview the Green Cricket, he will certainly think that by granting an interview he is taking precautions, but we are taking precautions, everyone plays his own game, as in Milligan. Do you follow me?"

Eighteen

WE ARE AT THE *Antártico*, A WELL-KNOWN ice-cream parlor at the mouth of the Douro, overlooking the splendid estuary of the river which traverses the city of Oporto. We have been granted an interview by a personage very much in the public eye, and on whom, according to certain witnesses, grave responsibilities appear to weigh in the matter of the death of Damasceno Monteiro. I refer to Sergeant Titânio Silva of the city Guardia Nacional, of whom we give the following profile in synopsis: fifty-four years of age, native of Felgueiras, of modest social background, enrolled in the National Guard at the age of nineteen, military training at Mafra, cadet in Angola from 1970 to 1973, decorated for valor during his military service in Africa, and for more than ten years, a sergeant at the Guardia Nacional headquarters in Oporto.

—*Sergeant, do you confirm the brief profile we have drawn of you? Are you a hero of the Portuguese campaigns in Angola?*

I do not think of myself as a hero, I simply did my duty to

my country and to the flag. To tell the truth, when I went to Angola I didn't even know the geography of the place. Let's say that it was in our overseas territories that I acquired my sense of patriotism.

—*Would you care to define what you mean by sense of patriotism?*

I mean that I realized I was fighting against people aiming to subvert our culture.

—*What do you mean by the word culture?*

Portuguese culture, of course, because that is what ours is.

—*And by the word subvert?*

I was referring to the blacks who shot at us because ordered to by individuals like Amílcar Cabral. I realized that I was defending territories which had been ours since time immemorial, when Angola had neither culture nor Christianity, both of which were brought there by us.

—*And then, having earned your medal, you came back home and started a career in the Oporto police.*

That is inexact. At first I was posted to the outskirts of Lisbon, and, since we had lost the war, we had to deal with all the jobless refugees returning from Africa, the *retornados*.

—*We who? Who had lost the war?*

We had, the Portuguese.

—*And how did things go with these people returning from the ex-colonies?*

There were a lot of problems, because they claimed the right to be put up in posh hotels. They even organized demonstrations and threw stones at the police. Instead of staying to defend Angola by force of arms they came to Lisbon and wanted to be kept in the lap of luxury.

—*And what was the next step in your career?*

I was transferred to Oporto. However, in the first place I was posted to Vila Nova de Gaia.

—*And rumor has it that at Gaia you established certain friendships.*

What do you mean by that?

—*We have heard tell of friendly relations with import-export firms.*

I think these are insinuations on your part. If you wish to make precise accusations then make them outright and I'll take you to court, because that's what you journalists deserve, to be hauled into court.

—*Come, sergeant, don't get all hot under the collar. I'm only speaking of rumors that have come to our ears. All the same we know that you had contacts with Stones of Portugal. Or do you think these also are mere insinuations? I repeat the question: do you or do you not know Stones of Portugal?*

I know them just as I know all the businesses operating in and around Oporto, and I knew they needed protection.

—*Why? Did it come to your knowledge that they had been threatened?*

Yes and no, even though the owner never explicitly complained of it. All the same we knew they needed surveillance because they imported hi-tech materials, delicate materials worth millions.

—*We are told that along with the hi-tech materials other merchandise arrived clandestinely in those containers. Did you know about this?*

I don't know what you're getting at.

—*Drugs. Pure heroin.*

If that had been the case we'd have known. We have first-rate sources of information.

—*In short you had no knowledge that drugs from Hong Kong arrived in the containers shipped to Stones of Portugal?*

No. Ours is a healthy city and doesn't need drugs. Our favorite thing is tripe.

—*All the same, we read in the nationwide Press that here in Oporto there's a nightclub where they peddle dope, and it appears that you own it.*

I firmly reject that insinuation. If you are referring to 'Puccini's Butterfly' let me tell you that it is frequented by people of class and distinction, and does not belong to me but to my sister-in-law, as duly registered with the proper municipal authorities.

—*However, it is said that you work there.*

I occasionally go and lend a hand with the accounting. I'm good at figures, I've done a course in administration.

—*But to return to the Stones of Portugal, it appears that that evening you were in the area on patrol with your squad, can you tell us about it?*

We arrived with our headlights dimmed, I don't recall the exact time but it must have been about midnight, it was only a spot-check.

—*What was the reason for this spot-check?*

I already told you that Stones of Portugal import hi-tech material, just the stuff to attract petty thieves, and our job is to protect it.

—*Go on.*

We parked the cars outside the gates and went in. The office light was on. I went in first and caught Damasceno Monteiro red-handed.

—*Could you clarify that statement?*

He was standing by the desk holding hi-tech material that he had certainly stolen.

—*Only such material and nothing else?*

Only such material.

—*Wasn't he also carrying some bags full of powder?*

I am a policeman, an official of the State, do you make so bold as to doubt my word?

—Perish the thought! What happened next?

We immediately arrested the subject, who thereafter re-vealed himself to be Monteiro. We ordered him to get into the car and took him to the station.

—At this point there emerges a contradiction between your two statements. According to our information, in your first state-ment you declared that you had let him out of the car in the course of the journey.

Who told you that?

—Let's simply say that the offices of the Public Prosecutor are always full of leaks; sometimes a typist, sometimes a switchboard operator, even a simple cleaning woman—but that's just by the way, the important thing is that in your first statement to the ex-amining magistrate you declared that Damasceno Monteiro had not been taken to the station at all, but had been put out of the car during the journey.

This is a misunderstanding which I took the trouble to clarify in person. A misunderstanding on the part of a col-league of mine, Officer Ferro.

—Can you give us a better explanation of this misunder-standing?

Our patrol was comprised of two cars. Monteiro was put into mine. The other car, driven by a colleague accompanied by Officer Ferro, followed behind. At a certain point we pulled up by the curb and Officer Ferro thought he had seen Senhor Monteiro alight from the car. But he was mistaken. I should make it clear that Officer Ferro is a recent recruit, a young fel-low, and you know what young men are, and it's easy to doze off in a car. He was simply mistaken.

—Nevertheless, in your statement to the examining magistrate you did not immediately question Officer Ferro's account.

I questioned it later, when I was able to study his account in detail.

—*Did you not in fact question that account because the witness, Senhor Torres, has sworn that he followed you in his car and with his own eyes saw his friend Damasceno kicked and beaten and dragged into the police station?*

Kicked and beaten?

—*That's what the witness says.*

My dear sir, we do not kick and beat people! Kindly set it down in black and white in your newspaper: we have all proper respect for the citizens of this country.

—*We place it on record that the conduct of the Guardia Nacional is irreproachable. But would you care to describe what happened that night?*

No trouble. We went up to the first floor, where the offices and detention room are, and set about a preliminary interrogation of the culprit. He appeared to be at the end of his tether, and burst into tears.

—*Did you touch him?*

Explain what you mean.

—*Did you lay hands on him physically?*

We don't lay hands on anyone, dear sir, because we respect the law and the Constitution, if you want to know. I simply tell you that Monteiro was beside himself and burst into tears. We even tried to comfort him.

—*You tried to comfort him?*

He was a poor devil, a pathetic creature, he cried out for his mother and said his father was an alcoholic. At that time there was only me and Officer Costa, because the other officer had gone to the lavatory, so I told Officer Costa to go downstairs to the kitchenette and brew up some coffee for him, because I really pitied that lad, I really did, so Officer Costa went down and a couple of minutes later he called upstairs and said: sergeant, come down, the machine doesn't work, the coffee won't go through. So I went downstairs too.

—*Leaving Damasceno Monteiro alone?*

Unfortunately, yes. That was our big mistake, for which we assume total responsibility: simply to make him some coffee we left that desperate lad alone for a few moments, and that is how the tragedy happened.

—*What tragedy? Could you explain yourself better?*

We heard a shot and dashed upstairs. Monteiro was lying lifeless on the floor. He had snatched up a revolver that the other officer had thoughtlessly left on the desk and shot himself through the temple.

—*Point-blank?*

When someone shoots themselves through the temple it's bound to be point-blank, don't you think?

—*Of course, I only asked in order to get an expert opinion, it's obvious that any suicide shoots himself point-blank. And then?*

Well, we found ourselves with that corpse on the floor. A thing like that, as you may readily understand, might throw a scare even into policemen thoroughly inured to the horrors of this world. Apart from that, I was on my last legs, I'd been on duty since eight in the morning, I had to get home and take an injection of Zomig.

—*Zomig?*

It's an American remedy which has only lately come on the market here, it's the only thing to relieve an unbearable attack of migraine. Attached to my legal statement is a medical certificate attesting to the migraine headaches I have been subject to ever since Angola, where a mine blew up right beside me and burst an eardrum. For that reason and that reason only did I leave my post, and that is the only offense, if it can be called an offense, which I shall have to answer for to the Court: that I fled the field, I who on the battlefield in Africa never left the field.

—And in so doing you left Damasceno Monteiro lying dead on the floor?

That's what happened. I don't know what my colleagues did after I left.

—Who were they?

I don't wish to give any names. I have already stated them to the examining magistrate and they will be mentioned at the trial.

—And what about the corpse of Damasceno Monteiro?

You must understand the anguish, the bewilderment of two poor recruits left with a corpse on the station floor. I make no excuses for them, but I can understand why they removed it.

—But this is a criminal act, called concealment of a corpse.

Certainly, I agree with you, it is concealment of a corpse, but I say again that you must understand the anguish of two simple recruits who find themselves in that sort of situation.

—When Damasceno Monteiro's body was found it had been decapitated.

Almost anything can happen in parks these days.

—You mean that when Damasceno's body was removed from the station it still had a head on it?

That is something which will emerge at the trial. As far as I am concerned I will swear by my boys. I can assure you that my subordinate officers are not head-hunters.

—You mean that in your opinion Monteiro's head was cut off in the park?

There's a lot of odd people around in the parks of this city.

—It would be difficult to accomplish such a feat in a park, according to the autopsy the beheading was an extraordinarily clean job, as if it had been done with an electric carving knife, and electric knives have to be plugged in.

If it comes to that there are butcher's knives that cut far cleaner even than an electric knife.

—*Nevertheless it has come to our knowledge that the body of Damasceno Monteiro bore signs of having been tortured. There were cigarette burns on his chest.*

We do not smoke cigarettes my dear sir, and you can put that down in your paper. No one smokes in my offices, I have expressly forbidden it, I have even put up notices to that effect on the walls. In any case you will have seen what the State has at last decided to print on every package of cigarettes? That smoking is seriously damaging to health.

Nineteen

"CONGRATULATIONS, YOUNG MAN, you did a good job there."

The lawyer was deep in his armchair under the book-shelves, in the room that morning there was an unusual fresh smell, a mixture of lavender and deodorant.

"Phew, what a stench," said Don Fernando, "the concierge has been in, she can't bear my cigars and I can't bear her wretched sprays."

Firmino noticed that the cards on the card table were all in stacks face upwards.

"Did you get out your game of patience?" he asked.

"This morning I did," replied the lawyer, "every so often I bring it off."

"That Titânio is a slimy character," observed Firmino. "The things he says, and the gall of the man!"

"Were you expecting anything better?" asked the lawyer, "It's the version he will stick to in court, and in those selfsame words, because this Titânio can plainly operate on only one stylistic level, however the records of trials are not published in the newspapers, but you have already let the reader know how the Green Cricket talks. And with this in my opinion your task is finished."

"Really finished?" asked Firmino.

"At least for the moment," replied the lawyer, "all the documents have been registered and the preliminary examination is closed, so we only have to wait for the trial. Which will be soon, perhaps sooner than you imagine, perhaps we will have occasion to meet again at the trial, who knows."

"You think it will come off so quickly?" asked Firmino.

"In cases such as this there are two possibilities," replied the lawyer, "the first is that they put off the trial until doomsday, so that people will forget, in the hope that some great national or international scandal will come along to occupy the whole attention of the press. The second is to resolve matters as soon as possible, and I think they will choose this second course, because they have to demonstrate that the course of justice is swift and efficient and that the public services, in this case the police, are transparently honest and above all democratic. You get the idea?"

"I get the idea," replied Firmino.

"Besides, you have a fiancée," continued the lawyer, "and one can't leave fiancées alone too long, otherwise they get dejected and pine. Go off and make love, it's one of the best things you can do at your time of life."

He turned his inquisitorial little eyes on Firmino as if expecting confirmation. Firmino felt himself blushing and gave a nod.

"And then there's your study of the post-war Portuguese novel, that's another task awaiting you, isn't it? Go back to Dona Rosa's and pack your bags, if you hurry there's a train at 2:18, but it's no great shakes, it stops even at Espinho, the next train is at 3:24, or else there are the 4:12 and the 6:10, take your pick."

"You certainly have the train times at your fingertips," said Firmino, "I imagine you travel that line pretty often."

"It's twenty-five years since I did so," replied the lawyer, "but I like train timetables, I find they have an intrinsic interest."

He got up and made for the bookshelves on one side of the room, where there were old books lavishly bound. He took out a slender volume bound in fine leather with silver-tipped corners, and held it out to Firmino. On the parchment fly-leaf was stamped the name of the bookbinder and a date: "Oficina Sampayo, Porto 1956." Firmino leafed through it. The cover of the original volume, which the binder had retained, was of stiffish paper, but yellowed with time, said in French, German, and Italian: Timetable of the Swiss Railways. Firmino examined it quickly and looked inquiringly at the lawyer.

"Many years ago," said Don Fernando, "when I was studying in Geneva, I bought that timetable, it was a commemorative publication of the Swiss railways, and the Swiss railways run on the dot as only the Swiss can make them, but the best of it is that they consider Zurich the center of the world, for example, turn to page four, after the advertisements for hotels and watches."

Firmino looked up page four.

"It's a map of Europe," he said.

"With all the railway lines," added Don Fernando, "each with its number, and each number refers to the lines in every country in Europe and the appropriate page. From Zurich you can reach the whole of Europe by train, and the Swiss railways indicate all the times for making your connection. For example, do you wish to go to Budapest? Turn to page sixteen."

Firmino looked for page sixteen.

"The train for Vienna leaves Zurich at 9:15 from platform 4, am I right?" said the lawyer. "The connection for Budapest, the best one, which is marked with an asterisk, is at 9 PM, it is the best because it enables one to catch the train coming from Venice, the timetable informs us of the services available, in this case couchettes for four persons (the cheapest), wagons-lits for two or private for one, restaurant car and possible light refreshments for the night. However, if you wish to go on to Prague, which is on the next page, you have only to choose between the various possibilities offered by the Hungarian railways, are you checking the text?"

"I'm checking it," said Firmino.

"Do you wish to visit the great northlands of Europe?" continued Don Fernando. "Oslo, for example, the city of the midnight sun and the Nobel Peace Prize: page nineteen, leaving Zurich at 12:21 from platform 7, the ferryboat timetable is provided in a footnote. Or, take your pick, it might be Magna Grecia, the Greek theater at Syracuse, the ancient culture of the Mediterranean, to get to Syracuse you only have to turn to page twenty-one, you leave Zurich at exactly 11 o'clock, and there you will find all the possible connections on the Italian railways."

"Have you made all these journeys?" asked Firmino.

Don Fernando smiled. He selected a cigar but did not light it.

"Naturally not," he replied, "I have simply confined myself to imagining them. After which I return to Oporto."

Firmino passed him the volume. Don Fernando took it, gave it a swift glance without opening it and handed it back.

"I know it by heart," he said, "I make you a present of it."

"But you may be attached to it," said Firmino, not knowing what else to say.

"Oh," said Don Fernando, "none of those trains run any more, that precise Swiss timing has been swallowed up by time itself. I give it to you as a souvenir of these days we've spent together, and a personal souvenir as well, if it is not presumptuous on my part to think that you might like to have something to remember me by."

"I shall keep it as a souvenir," replied Firmino. "And now please excuse me, Don Fernando, I have to get something, I'll be back in ten minutes."

"Leave the door on the latch," said the lawyer, "don't make me get up again to press the button."

FIRMINO RETURNED WITH A package under his arm. He undid it carefully and placed a bottle on the table.

"Before leaving I would like to drink a toast with you," he explained, "unfortunately the bottle isn't chilled."

"Champagne," observed Don Fernando, "it must have cost you a fortune."

"I chalked it up to my newspaper," admitted Firmino.

"I suspend judgment," said Don Fernando.

"With all the special editions they've printed thanks to our articles I think that the paper can treat us to a bottle of champagne."

"*Your* articles," specified Don Fernando as he fetched two glasses, "they were *your* articles."

"Well, anyway," murmured Firmino.

They raised their glasses.

"I propose we drink to the success of the trial," said Firmino.

Don Fernando took a sip and said nothing for the moment.

"Don't cherish too many hopes," he said as he put down his glass, "I'm prepared to bet it will be a military court."

"But that's ridiculous," exclaimed Firmino.

"It's logical according to the lawbooks," replied the lawyer phlegmatically, "the Guardia Nacional is a military body, I will do my best to challenge this logic, but I don't have too many hopes on that score."

"But this is a brutal murder," said Firmino, "a question of torture, of drug peddling, of corruption, it's got nothing to do with war."

"Of course, of course," murmured the lawyer, "and tell me, what's your fiancée called?"

"Catarina."

"A beautiful name," said the lawyer, "and what does she do in life?"

"She's just taken an exam for a post at the city library," said Firmino, "she's a graduate of library sciences, and a qualified archivist, but she's still waiting for the results."

"Working with books is a wonderful way of life," murmured the lawyer.

Firmino refilled the glasses. They sipped away in silence.

Finally Firmino picked up the bound volume and got to his feet.

"I think it's time I was going," he said.

They shook hands briefly.

"Give my best to Dona Rosa," Don Fernando called after him.

Firmino went out into Rua das Flores. A fresh breeze had sprung up, it almost had a nip in it. The air was as clear as crystal, he noted that the leaves of the plane-trees were patched here and there with yellow. It was the first sign of autumn.

Twenty

OF THAT DAY FIRMINO WAS destined to remember chiefly his physical sensations, lucid enough but as foreign to him as if he hadn't been involved at all, as if a protective film had cocooned him in a state between sleep and waking, where sensory perceptions are registered in the consciousness but the brain is powerless to organize them rationally, leaving them floating around as vague states of mind: that misty late-December morning when he arrived shivering with cold at the station in Oporto, the local trains unloading the early commuters with their faces still puffy with sleep, the taxi-ride by those sullen buildings of that damp and gloomy city. The whole place depressed him immensely. And then his arrival at the Law Courts, all that red tape at the entrance, the block-headed objections of the policeman at the door, who frisked him and wouldn't let him in with his pocket tape-recorder, his Union of Journalists' card which finally did the trick, his admittance to that tiny courtroom where all the seats were taken. He wondered why, for such an important trial, they had chosen such a small room, of course he knew the answer, although in that state of mingled insentience and hyper-awareness he was unable to articulate it mentally, and went no further than registering the fact.

He finally managed to find a place on the narrow dais reserved for the Press, segregated by a dark-stained, pot-bellied-columned balustrade. He had expected a crowd of reporters, photographers, flash-bulbs. But there was nothing of the sort. He recognized two or three colleagues, with whom he exchanged brief nods, but the rest were quite unknown to him, probably specialists in law cases. He realized that a lot of the newspapers would be falling back on information from press agencies.

In the front row he spotted Damasceno's parents. The mother was swathed in a grey coat and dabbed her eyes every so often with a crumpled handkerchief. The father was wearing an unbelievable red-and-black checked jacket, American style. To the right, at the table where the lawyers sat, he spotted Don Fernando. He had dumped his lawyer's gown on the table and was busy studying documents. He was wearing a black jacket and a white bow-tie. There were deep circles under his eyes and his lower lip drooped even more than usual. Between his fingers he was twisting an unlit cigar.

Leonel Torres was sitting practically huddled in his seat, looking scared out of his wits. Beside him sat a frail blonde who was presumably his wife. Sergeant Titânio Silva himself was seated with his two deputies. The latter were in uniform, whereas Titânio Silva, in mufti, was wearing a pin-striped suit and a silk tie. His hair was gleaming with brilliantine.

The Court entered and the proceedings began. Firmino thought of switching on his tape-recorder, but he had second thoughts because the courthouse had hopeless acoustics and the recording was sure to come out badly. Far better to take notes. He drew forth his notebook and wrote: The Missing Head of Damasceno Monteiro. After which he wrote no more, he just listened. He wrote nothing because he already knew all that was being said: the reading of Manolo the Gypsy's testimony about finding the body, the fisherman's statement that he had fished

up the head on the line he had out for chub, and the results of
the two autopsies. As to what Leonel Torres had to say, he knew
that as well, because the Judge simply asked him if he confirmed
what he had said during the preliminary investigations, and
Torres confirmed it. And when it came to Titânio Silva he too
confirmed his previous statement. His raven-black hair glis-
tened, his hair-line mustache kept time with the motion of his
thin lips. Of course, he said, his first statement to the examining
magistrates was the result of a misunderstanding, because the
young recruit who was with him in the car was sleepy, very
sleepy, poor lad, he had come on duty at six in the morning and
was only twenty years old, and at that age the body needs its
sleep, but yes, in fact they had taken Monteiro to the station,
and he was beside himself, at the end of his tether, he had bro-
ken down and cried like a child, he was a small-time crook, but
even crooks can sometimes touch the heart, so that he himself
and one of the deputies had gone down to the kitchenette on
the floor below to make him a cup of coffee.

The Judge remarked that for making a cup of coffee two
people seemed a little excessive. Well, true enough, or at least
it might seem to be true, replied the self-assured lips of Titânio
Silva in a sort of confidential whisper, but on the other hand
we have to consider the type of equipment the State supplies
to its commissariats, not that he wished to criticize the State,
he understood the difficulties of the State, the meager funds at
the disposal of the responsible ministry, but the fact was that
that coffee machine had been supplied nine years before, if the
Court wished to consult the Accounts Department it would
find all the invoices in the archives, and since for understand-
able reasons a nine-year-old coffee machine does not function
perfectly one has to work away at it, one has to turn up the gas
or turn down the gas, and so it happened that while he and the
deputy were working away at the machine, simply to get poor

Monteiro a cup of coffee, they heard a shot. They rushed upstairs, Monteiro was lying dead on the floor beside the desk,
with a pistol in his hand, the regulation pistol which the new
recruit Ferro had thoughtlessly left on the desk. Yes indeed, because even a police officer is not an automaton, even a police
officer can leave a pistol lying on a desk.

Of what followed Firmino only managed to memorize a
phrase or two here and there. He tried to pay as much attention as he could, but his mind, as if out of control, wandered
off on its own and dragged him back in time, out of that farce
of a courthouse, and without any logical sequence he felt himself now staring at a severed head placed in a dish, now in a
gypsy encampment on a suffocating August day, now in a
botanical garden gazing at a century-old exotic tree planted by
a lieutenant in Napoleon's army. And at that point they were
discussing Titânio Silva's migraines, and of this Firmino managed to take in a few scraps, the exhibiting of a medical certificate attesting to the fact that Sergeant Silva was affected by terrible migraine following the rupture of an eardrum caused by a
mine exploding near him in Angola, though he had never
claimed a State pension on those grounds, and because of this
ailment he had been obliged to go home for an injection of
Zomig, leaving the body of Monteiro there on the floor, after
which his two deputies began to stammer words to the effect
that yes, now they realized, now they understood that they
might be accused of the crime of concealment of a corpse, but
that evening their minds were far from the Penal Code, and in
any case neither of them knew a ruddy thing about the Penal
Code, they had just been so thunderstruck, and so damn
scared, that they'd removed the body and left it in a public
park.

When it came to the cigarette burns found on Monteiro's
body, Titânio Silva took it on himself to reply in person. And

while Firmino listened to his words, which were deadened as if by wads of cotton wool yet at the same time sharp, he realized he was beginning to sweat, as if he were on fire within, and all the time the thin lips of Titânio Silva were explaining to the Court with complete aplomb that he had had "No Smoking" notices put up all over the station, because as the scientists tell us and civilized countries have printed by law on every packet of cigarettes, smoking causes cancer. Someone in the court-room laughed inanely, and curiously enough that laugh struck Firmino as some kind of demented message, he realized that his hand was trembling slightly, but mechanically he wrote down: laughter in court.

And then the Judge, after the intervention of the Public Prosecutor, asked if Counsel wished to make any declaration before pronouncing their addresses to the Court. Counsel for the defense, a pot-bellied bumptious little man, announced that one thing had to be recorded in the acts of the proceedings, a question of principle, yes indeed, of nothing less than principle, his voice was curt and peremptory, Firmino tried to follow what he was saying, but as if his own mental integrity were at stake he felt threatened by those words and only managed to scribble down a few notes that now seemed to him disconnected: heroic conduct in the wars in Africa, bronze medal for military valor, devotion to the flag, lofty patriotism, the defense of true values, the struggle against crime, perfect trust in the State and Nation.

There followed an interval of no more than a few seconds, to Firmino it seemed endless, a sort of limbo during which his memory carried him back to a white house on the shore at Cascais and his father's face, to a blue sea with white-crested waves, to a wooden Pinocchio doll with whom an infant Firmino had his bath in a zinc tub on a terrace. The Judge said: The prosecution has the floor. Don Fernando rose, negli-

gently, put on his gown, carried himself over to beneath the
Bench and surveyed the public. His face was a pasty yellow.
His pendulous cheeks hung down on either side of his face like
the ears of a basset-hound. In his hand was his unlit cigar, and
with that cigar he indicated a point in the ceiling as if aiming
at someone in particular.

"I will start with a question which I address chiefly to myself," said Don Fernando. "What does it mean to be against
death?"

At that moment Firmino pressed the button on his tape
recorder.

THE TRAIN RUMBLED ON through the darkness. Out of
the window Firmino saw a cluster of distant lights. Maybe it
was Espinho. He'd taken a seat in the restaurant car, which in
fact was nothing but a self-service with a couple of tables at
one end. Behind the counter stood a waiter, a weary look on
his face and a cloth in his hand. He approached Firmino.

"I'm sorry, sir, but you can't stay here without taking
refreshment."

"Bring me whatever you like," said Firmino, "perhaps a
cup of coffee."

"The machine is switched off sir," said the waiter.

"In that case a glass of mineral water."

"I am sorry," said the waiter "but I cannot serve you anything because the restaurant is closed."

"So what's to be done?" asked Firmino.

"You cannot stay here without ordering something,"
repeated the waiter, "but you cannot order anything."

"I don't follow the logic," retorted Firmino.

"It's Company regulations," explained the waiter placidly.

"But what do you have to do now?" enquired Firmino
tactfully.

"I have to clean up sir," said the waiter, "I'm supposed to be only a waiter, because that's what's written in my contract, but the Company makes me do the cleaning up as well, and my union doesn't stick up for me."

"Very well then," said Firmino, "while you are cleaning up let me sit here, I won't give you any trouble, we can keep each other company."

The waiter gave a comprehending nod and went off. Firmino fished out his notepad and tape-recorder. He thought about how to write his article about the trial. He hadn't taken notes, but for the general drift he could trust to his memory. As for Don Fernando's speech he had it in that little contraption, and even if the recording was defective it could be transcribed with a bit of effort. More lights came into view through the window. La Granja? Dammit, he couldn't remember whether La Granja came before or after Espinho.

Darkness pressed on the window-panes. He got out his pen and prepared to take shorthand. He thought that one doesn't realize it at the time, but everything in life can come in useful, even that shorthand course he had taken long ago. He hoped he was still fast enough and pressed the button to start.

The voice seemed to come from far away. The recording was very faulty, the words drifted off into nothing.

". . . question I address chiefly to myself: what does it mean to be against death?...

....

.... every man is absolutely indispensable to to all the others and all are absolutely indispensable to each ....

....

.... and all are beings in a human

sense leading to him, each man is the root of the human essence .... I repeat, the human essence of man is the point of reference .... the ethical affirmation is originally aimed against the negation of man, therefore the fact of his being against death is a positive thing in man, but since man has no experience of his own death, only that of others, in the light of which he can only imagine and fear his own .... and it is the ultimate basis and insuperable condition of any humanistic ethic, that is of any .... ”
....

The waiter came up and Firmino switched off the machine.

"Listening to the radio?" asked the waiter.

"No," answered Firmino, "it's a recording I made this morning, it's a law case."

"If it's a law case it must be interesting," said the waiter, "I once saw a trial on television and it was just like a film."

Then he added: "If you want to stay here you've got to eat or drink something."

"And if I did?" asked Firmino, "what if I did eat something?"

"You can't, it's against Company regulations."

"Have you any idea who the Railway Company is?" retorted Firmino.

The man appeared to give the matter some thought. He propped his broom against the side of the carriage.

"To tell you the truth I only know Senhor Pedro, who's the bloke at the window in the personnel office."

"And do you think this Senhor Pedro is the Railway Company personified?"

"Not likely," replied the waiter, "in any case he's due for a pension."

"In that case why not have something to eat," said Firmino, "we could even eat together at this very table, and what'd you say to something hot, eh?"

The waiter scratched his head.

"The coffee machine's off," he said, "but we could switch on the electric hotplates."

"Good idea," declared Firmino, "and what could we cook on the hotplates?"

"What would you say to scrambling each of us a couple of eggs?" suggested the waiter.

"With ham?" prompted Firmino.

"With ham from Trás-os-Montes!" declared the waiter, moving off.

Firmino switched on the recorder again.

"*Es ist ein eigentümlicher Apparat*, this is an odd sort of machine. These words were written way back in 1914 by an unknown Jew, born in Prague, but who wrote in German ....

....
.... a very odd sort of machine that perpetuates a barbarous law ....

....
.... perhaps the machine of a penal colony or a terrible prediction of the monstrous event

which Europe was due to witness?..
....
.... monstrous, *ungeheuer*, the monster and vampire
concealed behind the *Grundnorm*...
....
.... writing there in Prague he could scarcely
know what the people in whose language he wrote would later
commit ....
....
.... because it is evident that murder is
not enough ....
torture...
....
the jailers ....
.... before killing a man you
have to inflict pain, to savage him, to lacerate the flesh of
a man ....
.... are we to claim,
you and I, that none of us is responsible for this abiding monstrosity of human history? But what then becomes of individual responsibility, for torture, one of the theoretical bases of
monstrosity? ...."

More incomprehensible buzzing, with background noises
and mutterings from the public. Firmino pressed the STOP
button. The waiter arrived with a steaming pan of scrambled
eggs and buttered toast. He proceeded to set the table.

"Did you switch it off?" he asked.

"I can't hear much, worse luck, and when he turns towards
the Bench his voice gets completely lost in the sound of electronic crackle."

"Who's it talking?" asked the waiter.

"A lawyer in Oporto," replied Firmino, "but you can only catch a phrase here and there."

"May I listen in?" asked the waiter.

Firmino pressed the button.

". . . therefore if I may be permitted a literary allusion, because literature also is an aid to understanding law .... the *machines célibataires* as the French Surrealists called them, the things most deadly to life .... our police stations today, in this year of grace in which we live, are our *machines célibataires* .... the needles they use in penal colonies or merely cigarettes stubbed out on the naked flesh .... reading the reports of the inspectors appointed by the Council of Europe for Human Rights relating to places of detention in our so-called civilized countries ....a blood-curdling document dealing with places of detention in Europe ...."

The old lawyer's voice was lost in a sort of gurgle.

"He was too far away," said Firmino, "and worse still he sometimes lowers his voice and almost mumbles to himself."

"Try again," said the waiter.

Firmino pressed the START button.

". . . a great contemporary writer has interpreted that prophetic narrative written in 1914, arriving at the humanistic conclusions with which I opened this speech .... if it is true, as he asserts, that that narrative succeeded in giving body and meaning to the phantoms of regret .... but what sort of nostalgia are we speaking of? Some paradise lost, a nostalgia for purity, a time when man was not yet contaminated by evil? we are not in a position to say, but we can assert with Camus that the great revolutions are always metaphysical and that, as he affirms by referring to Nietzsche, the great Problems are to be found by the roadside .... this man who stands before us, and whom I have not the least compunction in calling ignoble, on account of the tortures he practices, because surely no one can imagine anybody stubbing out cigarettes on a corpse, so .... our police stations without any legal control and protection, where individuals such as Sergeant Titânio Silva operate. .... "

More incomprehensible noises were heard and Firmino switched off the tape-recorder.

"Time to eat these eggs," said the waiter.

"They're still warm," replied Firmino.

"Like a spot of ketchup?" asked the waiter, "everyone asks for ketchup nowadays."

"I can do without," said Firmino.

"What he said about the big problems being found by the roadside really struck me I must say," said the waiter, "who was it who wrote that?"

"Albert Camus," replied Firmino, "he was a French writer, but in fact he was quoting a German philosopher."

"About this lawyer," said the waiter, "what's his name?"

"It's a bit long and complicated," said Firmino," but there in Oporto everyone calls him Attorney Loton."

"Press the button again, I'd like to hear more of what he has to say."

Firmino pressed the button.

"...and as for the supposed suicide of Damasceno Monteiro ....
.... Jean Améry
....
.... his implacable pages, *Diskurs über den Freitod*, tell us that abhorrence of life is the basic prerequisite for a voluntary death, though not only his book but the story of his life is essential to our understanding ....
....
.... Jean Améry, a Mittel-European Jew, was born in Vienna, took refuge in Belgium in the late 1930s, was deported by the Germans in 1940, escaped from the concentration camp of Gurs and joined the Belgian Resistance, arrested by the Nazis again in 1943, tortured by the Gestapo and sent to Auschwitz, he survived ....
....
.... but what is the meaning of survival?
....
.... I ask myself
....
.... devoting himself with great finesse to literature he wrote in both German and French, I recall for example his studies on Flaubert and two novels ....

....
.... but can writing save one from an
irreparable humiliation? ....
....
.... he finally committed suicide in
Salzburg in 1978 ....
....
.... and I therefore assert that if Damasceno Monteiro laid violent hands upon himself, because my
profound doubts in the matter cannot be confirmed by any
witness, even though we have to strain all reason to credit this
version of the facts ....
....
.... his desperate act would have been forced upon
him, as the result of the tortures he had undergone, as shown
by the results of the autopsy ....
....
.... I assert that the person responsible is Sergeant Titânio Silva ....
....
.... the methods worthy of the Inquisition employed in his
headquarters ....
....
.... do my opinions strike you as Quixotic? In
that case allow me one last literary quotation, in saying that
for all essential questions, by which I mean those for which
people risk death, or which strengthen the will to live, there
are only two ways of thought, that of Don Quixote and that of
Monsieur La Palisse ....
....
.... they would have us believe that Damasceno
Monteiro died on account of a cup of coffee ....
....

.... but this insulting idiocy, worthy indeed of Monsieur La Palisse, which we have heard in the laughable testimony of the accused, stops nothing short of infamy, ...

yes infamy, ...

.... and I will attempt to explain what I mean by infamy ...."

Firmino pressed the STOP button.

"After this the recording is even more of a washout," he said, "but I assure you that from here on the lawyer's speech was something to send shivers down your spine, I should have taken it down in shorthand at the time, but I'm not fast enough, and in any case I put my faith in this contraption."

"That's a shame," said the waiter, "what happened next?"

"We come to his winding up," said Firmino, "in which he recalled the Salsedo case."

"What was that?" asked the waiter.

"I didn't know either," replied Firmino, "but it was something that happened in the United States, during the 1930s, I think, Salsedo was an anarchist who was pushed out of a police station window and the police made it out to be suicide, the case was revealed to the world by a lawyer who I think was called Galleani, and that was the end of the speech, but as you can hear there's nothing left on the tape."

The waiter got to his feet.

"In a while we'll be arriving at Lisbon," he said, "I must go and get my things together."

"Make me out a bill," said Firmino, "I'm paying for both of us."

"That's impossible," objected the waiter, "I'd have to ring it up on the cash register, which also registers the time, and that would show that you've eaten at a time when one can't eat."

"I don't follow the logic," replied Firmino.

"Four scrambled eggs won't ruin the Company," said the waiter, "and it was nice to have someone to chat to, the journey seemed shorter, I'm only sorry about your recording, goodbye now."

Firmino replaced the tape-recorder in his case and glanced through the notepad left open on the table. It was blank. The only thing he had managed to scribble down was the sentence. He re-read it.

"This Court, in virtue of the powers conferred on it by Law, having duly examined the evidence and heard the accused and Counsel for the defense and prosecution, condemns officers Costa and Ferro to two years of imprisonment for the charge of concealment of a corpse and failure to report aggravated by the fact that these offenses were committed by public officials in the exercise of their duties. However, the Court grants probation. It finds Sergeant Silva guilty of negligence in having left the station during duty hours, and suspends him from service for six months. It finds him not guilty of murder."

The first lights of the outskirts began to twinkle through the carriage window. Firmino picked up his case and went out into the corridor. Not a soul in sight. He glanced at his watch. The train was on the dot.

Twenty-One

FIRMINO STEPPED OUT OF THE Faculty of Letters and halted at the top of the steps to scan the parking lot for Catarina. April was glittering in all its glory. Firmino looked at the trees in the large square of this university town bursting with early spring foliage.

He took off his jacket, it was almost hot enough to be summer. Then he spotted her car and started down the steps brandishing a sheet of paper.

"You can start packing," was his triumphant cry, "we're off!"

Catarina threw her arms around his neck and kissed him.

"When do we start?"

"At once. In theory even tomorrow."

"For a whole year?"

"The whole year's grant went to the chap who was in a class by himself," said Firmino, "but they've given me six months, which is better than nothing, don't you think?"

He rolled down the car window and murmured dreamily: "L'Arc de Triomphe, the Champs-Elysées, the Musée d'Orsay, the Bibliothèque Nationale, the Latin Quarter—six months in the 'Ville Lumière'—don't you think we should celebrate?"

"Yes, let's celebrate," replied Catarina, "but are you sure the money will be enough for two?"

"The monthly grant comes to quite a bit," replied Firmino, "of course Paris is a fiercely expensive city, but I also have the right to substantial meal tickets at the students' canteen, it won't be a life of luxury but we'll get by."

Catarina edged her way in to the traffic in Campo Grande. "Where shall we go to celebrate?" she asked.

"Maybe at 'Tony das Bifes,'" suggested Firmino, "however first go round the roundabout and take me to the office, I want to settle things at once with the Editor, and in any case it's still only midday."

THE SWITCHBOARD LADY IN HER wheelchair was already having her meal out of a small tinfoil dish and reading a weekly magazine she was particularly fond of.

"There you are, reading all our trade rivals," teased Firmino in passing.

That morning the editorial staff was present in full strength. Firmino led Catarina through the maze of desks, gave Silva an amiable "Good morning, Monsieur Huppert", rapped twice on the Editor's glass door, and breezed right in.

"My fiancée," announced Firmino.

"How d'you do," murmured the Editor.

They sat themselves down on those agonizing white metal chairs which the Modernist architect had scattered everywhere. As usual the fug in the Editor's office was unfit to breathe.

"I have a little matter I wish to discuss with you, sir," said Firmino, not quite knowing how to begin. But then he charged in with: "I want to ask for six months' leave."

The Editor lit a cigarette, gave Firmino a blank look and said: "Explain yourself better."

Firmino set out to explain everything as best he could: the scholarship he had won, the chance of research work in Paris under a professor at the Sorbonne, and of course he would give up his salary, but if he left the paper he would be without social security, he didn't ask the paper to pay his monthly installments, he'd do that out of his own pocket, it was just that he didn't want to find himself in the position of being unemployed, because as the Editor very well knew, here in Portugal the unemployed were fobbed off with about enough to starve a stray dog, and in any case in six months' time he'd be back at work again, cross his heart he would.

"Six months is a long time," muttered the Editor, "and who knows how many cases will come our way in the next six months?"

"Think of it this way," replied Firmino, "summer is on the doorstep, the holidays will soon be starting and people will be off to the seaside, it seems that people kill each other less in summertime, I've read it in some statistic or other, and maybe the job of special correspondent could be taken over by Senhor Silva, he's really been panting for it."

The Editor said nothing. He appeared to be thinking it over. Meanwhile Firmino had a sudden inspiration.

"Hey, I could send you reports from Paris, that's a city with a mass of *crimes passionels*, it's not every paper that can afford a special correspondent in Paris, and you'd have one free of charge. Just think how posh it would sound: from our special correspondent in Paris."

"That might be a solution," replied the Editor, "but I have to give it some thought, we'll discuss the matter calmly tomorrow, and in the meanwhile let me think it over."

Firmino got up to go. Catarina got up with him.

"Ah, one moment," said the Editor, "there's a telegram for you, arrived yesterday."

He handed over the telegram and Firmino opened it. It read: "Must speak to you urgently Stop Expect you tomorrow

178 • ANTONIO TABUCCHI

in my library Stop Useless telephone me Stop Best wishes
Fernando de Mello Sequeira."

Firmino read the telegram and gave Catarina a worried
look. She returned it with a questioning air. Firmino read the
telegram out loud.

"What does he want me for?" he asked.

Neither of them had anything to say.

"What shall I do?" asked Firmino, turning to Catarina.

"I think you ought to go."

"You really do?" insisted Firmino.

"Why not? After all," smiled Catarina, "Oporto isn't the
end of the world."

"What about our celebration at 'Tony dos Bifes'?" asked
Firmino.

"We can put that off until tomorrow," answered Catarina,
"let's just have a snack at the 'Versailles' and then I'll take you
to the station. It's ages since I've been to the 'Versailles.'"

HOW DIFFERENT IS A CITY seen in the broad light of
day and in blazing sunshine. Firmino cast his mind back to the
last time he had seen that city, that misty December day when
everything had seemed so dreary and dreadful. But now
Oporto wore a gladsome look, lively, animated and the potted
flowers on the sills of Rua das Flores were all in bloom.

Firmino pressed the bell and the door clicked open. He
found Don Fernando sprawled on the sofa under the book-
shelves. He was in a dressing gown, as if he had only just got
out of bed, but wore a silk scarf round his neck.

"Good evening, young man," he said vaguely, "thank you
for coming, make yourself at home."

Firmino sat down.

"You wanted to see me urgently," he said, "what's it all
about?"

"We'll discuss that later," said Don Fernando, "first tell me about yourself and your fiancée, how is she, have they taken her on at the library?"

"Not yet," replied Firmino.

"And your thesis on the post-war novel in Portugal?"

"I've written it," said Firmino, "but it's not very long, just a brief essay of twenty-odd pages."

"Still on your beloved Lukács?" enquired Don Fernando.

"I've adjusted my sights a little," explained Firmino, "I concentrated on a single novel and incorporated other methods."

"Tell me all," said the lawyer.

"Newspaper weather reports as a metaphor of prohibition in a 1960s Portuguese novel, that's what I've called my dissertation."

"And a very fine title too," said the lawyer approvingly. "And on whose method do you base it?"

"Mostly on Lotman, as regards decoding the secret message," explained Firmino, "but I've kept in Lukács as far as politics are concerned."

"An interesting mélange," said the lawyer, "I should like to read it, perhaps you might send me a copy. Anything else to tell me?"

"On the basis of this work I put in for a scholarship to go to Paris, and I won it," Firmino admitted with some measure of pride. "I have a really good research project under way."

"Very interesting," said the lawyer, "and what's your project about?"

"Censorship in literature," said Firmino.

"Is that the case!" exclaimed the lawyer, "I offer my congratulations. And when do you hope to leave?"

"The sooner the better," replied Firmino, "the grant starts the moment the candidate accepts, and I signed the acceptance form this morning."

"I see," said the lawyer, "in that case I may have brought you here to no purpose, I didn't bargain on an event so gratifying yet so demanding on you."

"Why to no purpose?" enquired Firmino.

"I had need of your help."

Don Fernando got up and made his way to the desk. There he selected a cigar and inhaled its odor for a long time without making up his mind to light it, then he flopped down on the sofa again, threw his head back and gazed at the ceiling.

"I'm asking for a retrial," he said.

Firmino stared at him in astonishment.

"But it's too late now," he said, "you didn't appeal within the legal time-limit."

"That is true," admitted the lawyer, "at that time it seemed useless."

"And the case has been closed," Firmino pointed out.

"True, it has been closed," said the lawyer. "And I shall have it reopened."

"On what grounds?" asked Firmino.

Don Fernando said nothing, but pulled himself upright, and without getting up opened a small buffet beside the sofa, extracting a bottle and two glasses.

"It's not an exceptional port," he said, "but it has its dignity."

He poured out the wine and at last made up his mind to light the cigar.

"I have an eyewitness," he said almost in a whisper, "and the things he witnessed justify me in asking for a retrial."

"An eyewitness?" repeated Firmino, "but how do you mean?"

"An eyewitness to the murder of Damasceno Monteiro," replied Don Fernando.

"Who is it?"

"The name is Wanda," said the lawyer, "a person I happen to know."

"Wanda who?"

The lawyer took a sip of port.

"Wanda is a poor creature," he replied, "one of those poor creatures who rove the face of the earth and have no hope of the kingdom of heaven. Eleutério Santos, known as Wanda. A transvestite."

"I don't see where this is getting us," said Firmino.

"Eleutério Santos," continued Don Fernando, as if reciting a crime-sheet, "thirty-two years old, born in a village in the mountains of the Marao to a family of very poor shepherds, sexually abused by an uncle at eleven years old, raised in a Home until seventeen years of age, occasional jobs like unloading fruit at the mouth of the Douro, other occasional work as assistant grave-digger at the public cemetery, a year in mental hospital here in Oporto suffering from depression, a sojourn which obliged him to live cheek by jowl with oligophrenics and schizophrenics in those exemplary hospices on which our country so prides itself, at present simply Wanda, known to the police as a prostitute walking the streets of Oporto, with the occasional slight depressive crisis, though now he can afford to see a doctor."

"You certainly know all about him," observed Firmino.

"I was his legal adviser in a case against a casual client who slashed him during an encounter in a car," said Don Fernando, "a petty sadist who however had a bit of money, and Wanda didn't come out of it too badly."

"And the evidence?" asked Firmino, "tell me about the evidence."

"To put it briefly," replied Don Fernando, "Wanda was on his usual street, but that evening it seems there wasn't much in the way of business, so she moved to a side street that wasn't in her territory and there ran into the pimp who controls that street, who flew at her at once. Wanda defended herself and there was a scuffle. A patrol of the Guardia Nacional came by, the pimp took to his heels leaving Wanda flat out on the ground, they shoved her into the car, took her to the police station and put her in the detention cell, or rather, what they call the detention cell but is really only an ordinary little room adjoining the offices. However it happened that those particular patrolmen had a proper sense of duty and registered the fact that Wanda had been taken into custody. The register clearly states: Eleutério Santos, entry 2300 hours. And there is no way they can tamper with that register."

The lawyer fell silent while he filled the air with puffs of smoke and gazed once more at the ceiling.

"Then what?" asked Firmino.

"The patrol which had arrested Wanda went off duty and Wanda was left in the little room which, as I have said, adjoined the offices, and there she lay down on a bunk and went to sleep. At about half-past twelve she was awakened by cries, she opened the door a crack and peeped through. There was Damasceno Monteiro."

The lawyer paused to put out his cigar. His little eyes in their pouches of fat were focused on a point in the distance.

"They had tied him to a chair, he was stripped to the waist and Sergeant Titânio Silva was stubbing out cigarettes on his belly. Seeing that there's No Smoking in that police station, Damasceno Monteiro provided a convenient ashtray. This Titânio wanted to know who had stolen the previous consignment of heroin, because this was the second time he'd been ripped off and Damasceno swore he didn't know, that this was the first time he had done a job at Stones of Portugal. And at a certain point Damasceno started yelling that he'd denounce him, that the whole town would know it was Sergeant Titânio

Silva who controlled all the heroin peddling in Oporto, and this Titânio started to jibber and jump up and down like a madman, though these details are superfluous, you'll learn more about them later, until he pulled out his pistol and shot the lad point-blank through the temple."

The lawyer poured himself out another glass of port.

"Does the story interest you?" he asked.

"Very much so," replied Firmino, "and how does it go on?"

"This Titânio told officer Costa to go down to the kitchen and fetch the electric carving knife. Costa came back with the knife and Titânio said: 'Cut off his head, Costa, he's got a bullet in his brain that would give us away, you go and throw the head into the river while Ferro and I take care of the body.'"

The lawyer glanced at him with his little restless eyes and asked: "Satisfied?"

"Very much so," said Firmino, "but where do I come into it?"

"Look here," said Don Fernando, "I already know all these details, but I can't get them into the papers. And as this morning I took Wanda to give evidence to the appropriate authorities, I would like her to repeat what she knows to a newspaper, let us call it a sort of precaution, in view of all the road accidents that happen in this country."

"I take your point," said Firmino, "where can I find this Wanda?"

"I've put her into hiding at my brother's farm, she'll be safe there," said Don Fernando.

"When can I interview her?" asked Firmino.

"At once if you like, but it would be better if you went on your own, if you wish I will telephone to Manuel to take you in my car."

"Fine," said Firmino.

The lawyer rang Manuel.

"The time it will take him to get the car out of the garage," he said as he hung up, "not more than ten minutes."

"I'll go out and wait for him in the street," said Firmino, "the air is especially pleasant today, have you smelt the sweet scent of spring, Don Fernando?"

"What about your scholarship?" asked Don Fernando.

"There's time for that," said Firmino, "it lasts six months, if I lose a day or so it won't matter, later on I'll give my girl a call."

He opened the door to leave, but paused on the threshold.

"You know, no one is going to believe that evidence."

"You think not?"

"A transvestite," said Firmino, "psychiatric hospitals, known to the police as a prostitute. Just imagine."

AND HE MADE TO CLOSE THE door behind him. Don Fernando raised a hand to stop him. He heaved himself to his feet and advanced into the middle of the room. He pointed at the ceiling, as if addressing the air, then pointed a finger at Firmino, then stabbed a thumb at his own chest.

"She's a human being," he said, "remember that, young man, first and foremost she's a human being."

He paused, then went on: "Try to be gentle with her, be very tactful, Wanda is a creature as fragile as crystal, one word out of place and she bursts into tears."

Helsinki, 30 *October* 1996

Note

The characters, locations and situations here described are purely the fruit of the author's imagination. From actual fact he has drawn one very tangible episode which set that imagination in motion: on the night of May 7, 1966, Carlos Rosa, twenty-five years old, a Portuguese citizen, was killed in a police station of the Republican National Guard at Sacavém on the outskirts of Lisbon, and his body was found in a public park, decapitated and showing evidence of torture.

For certain themes of a legal nature to be found in this book I owe much to friendly conversations with Judge Antonio Cassese, president of the International Penal Court of Justice at the Hague, as well as reflections arising from his book *Umano-Disumano. Commissariati e prigioni nell'Europa di oggi* (*Inhuman States. Imprisonment, Detention and Torture in Europe Today*, Polity Press, Cambridge, 1995).

This novel is also indebted to the person whom I here call Manolo the Gypsy, a fictional character, if you like, though it would be better to say a whole community concentrated in one individual in a story to which, on the plane of what is called reality, he is extraneous. Far from extraneous to the story, however, are certain unforgettable tales heard told by old gypsies one far-off afternoon at Janas, during the blessing of the animals, in the days when the nomad people still had horses.

I wish to thank Danilo Zolo for all the information regarding the philosophy of law which he was kind enough to provide me with, and Paola Spinesi and Massimo Marianetti for the care and patience with which they transformed the original manuscript into a typewritten text.

It only remains to add that Damasceno Monteiro is the name of a street in a working-class district of Lisbon where I once happened to live, and that the opening sentences of Loton's speech for the prosecution are taken from the philosopher Mario Rossi. The rest of that speech relies solely on the culture and convictions of the character himself.

A.T.